KILLER'S GUN

KILLER'S GUN

RAY HOGAN

THORNDIKE
CHIVERS

This Large Print edition is published by Thorndike Press, Waterville, Maine, USA and by AudioGO Ltd, Bath, England.

Thorndike Press, a part of Gale, Cengage Learning.

LIBRARY OF CONGRESS CATALOGING-IN-PUBLICATION DATA

Hogan, Ray, 1908–1998.
    Killer's gun / by Ray Hogan. — Large print ed.
        p. cm. — (Thorndike Press large print western)
    ISBN-13: 978-1-4104-3989-5 (hardcover)
    ISBN-10: 1-4104-3989-5 (hardcover)
    1. Large type books. I. Title.
PS3558.O3473K55 2011
813'.54—dc23   2011022658

BRITISH LIBRARY CATALOGUING-IN-PUBLICATION DATA AVAILABLE

Published in 2011 in the U.S. by arrangement with Golden West Literary Agency.

Published in 2012 in the U.K. by arrangement with Golden West Literary Agency.

U.K. Hardcover: 978 1 445 86049 7 (Chivers Large Print)
U.K. Softcover: 978 1 445 86050 3 (Camden Large Print)

Printed in the United States of America
1 2 3 4 5 6 7 15 14 13 12 11

KILLER'S GUN

I

Luke Wade slouched against the wall of Red Hill's largest saloon, *The Wagonmaster,* and stared moodily into the distance beyond the dusty street. So far it had been another wild goose chase — and he was almost broke again. He stirred impatiently, frustration racking his mind and etching deep lines in his browned features. He guessed he would have to find himself a job, stick with it long enough to accumulate some cash — and then take up the search once more.

A lean, gray-eyed, remote sort of young man, he pulled in his glance, allowed it to drift down the drab, narrow channel lying between the rows of weathered buildings. It was mid-morning and several persons moved along the plank walks, getting their business out of the way before the driving heat set in. According to the remarks he had heard since reaching Red Hill, it was unseemly hot for so early in the summer —

what the hell; it was hot in summer everywhere, and every year.

His gaze halted on a buggy drawn up in front of *Copp's General Store.* A rancher, no doubt, who might possibly have room in his crew for another man. Two buckboards were in the wagonyard at the side of *Marmon's Hay & Grain Company.* Prospects, also.

Elsewhere along the street a few saddled horses dozed at hitchracks, and the town marshal, his star glinting in the sunlight, lounged in the open doorway of his office. The old lawman had watched him closely ever since he had arrived in Red Hill; but that was always the pattern so far as Luke was concerned and he had grown accustomed to the cold, hard stare of lawmen during the past three years.

Perhaps it was the grim, humorless set of his face, or maybe the flat depths of his eyes that drew their immediate suspicion, telegraphed to them that here walked trouble and sudden death. Or it could have been the heavy, ornate .45 worn low on his thigh. Regardless which, they would have guessed right — and Luke Wade reckoned he had good reason to be the sort of man he was.

It had begun three years ago, up in the lonely Chugwater country of Wyoming. There had been a ranch — a small one, to be sure, but one gaining ground as the months passed. He and his father, Ben, crippled by the war, had worked it alone. Things had looked promising, and Luke, on the very day he'd turned twenty, had ridden in to Laramie to meet with a cattle buyer and arrange for the sale of their small herd.

It had taken longer than he'd expected, and by the time he'd had purchase details arranged and other matters settled, ten days had gone by. And then when he'd finally returned home he had found his father dead — murdered, their house burned to the ground and the cattle gone.

Ben Wade had not died easily or quickly. Luke had found him near the well, two bullet wounds in his breast. Nearby had lain his old cavalry saber. With a faltering hand Luke's father had scrawled a message on the back of an envelope he had been carrying. Luke still carried the note.

Solong son. Hate not seeing you but I reckon this is the way it was meant to be. Three men done it. Not Indians. Jumped me about dark same day you left. Strangers. Cut one with old Betsy. Nipple to hip. Not deep but he'll have a long scar. Big man. Then he shot me. Fancy gun. Wish I

There the painful, almost illegible scrawl had trailed off, leaving to Luke Wade a heritage of hate that had increased rather than diminished as the years had passed.

He had little to go on — a big man with a long scar across his belly, and who had dropped his pistol during the encounter. Slashed by the saber, he had apparently shot Ben Wade, then staggered back clutching his wound. In the process he had lost his weapon and, not noticing, ridden on. Luke, hunting about for more evidence, had discovered it half buried in the sand, its blood-spattered, delicately carved handles with their silver inlays glinting in the sunlight.

So for three years Luke had been drifting back and forth across the frontier in a grim quest, always looking for a man with such a scar, and forever watching for reaction in a rider's eyes that would betray recognition of the ornate .45 — the killer's gun.

That winter he had been in New Mexico's Seven Rivers country, near the Pecos. A tip from a drover had turned him west to Red Hill and an area known as the Mangus Valley — he had seen a man with a scar across his middle, the drover had said. There had been a saloon fight, and the man — a rancher, he thought he was — had stepped in to halt it, and gotten his shirt ripped for his efforts. The drover had been sure it had been in Red Hill . . . well, pretty sure. Man saw a lot of saloon brawls, knocking around the country.

But it was a lead, and Luke followed them all. He was hardened to disappointment after all this time, and he recognized the difficulty of locating the killer for whom he searched. Such a scar would always be hidden from casual glance — and a man could mask his surprise at seeing a weapon he had lost under the circumstances involved. Luke could have faced the killer a dozen times and never known it. But the search had become a grim, bitter way of life for him, and he wasn't going to give it up.

Now he was in the broad, gleaming southwestern corner of New Mexico, bordering on the new, born-of-war territory of Arizona. It was new country. Ranches had begun to spring up here in only the last three or four years, and possibilities, because of that fact, were good. It could mean nothing, or it could mean much; if the killer had been no more than a common rustler who'd taken the Wade herd for the immediate cash it would bring, he would be wasting time.

However, if the murderer of Ben Wade were a ruthless man out to build up a ranch quickly for himself, he could very well be one of those newcomers who had settled in Mangus Valley. Chugwater was far away, and the time element was right. . . .

But the quest would have to grind to a halt, for now. A man had to eat, and to eat he had to work.

Luke reached into his pocket and brought forth the few coins he possessed. About five dollars, he saw, making a casual count. Enough to buy a drink or two and eat for a couple of days. By then he should have a job located. Ranchers were hiring this time of the year. He threw a glance at the buggy and saw that it was still unattended. He could talk to the owner later; meanwhile, he'd go inside and jaw with the bartender. Bartenders usually knew everything that was going on.

He wheeled, and came into hard collision with one of three men emerging from the saloon. The impact knocked the nearest of the trio, a squat, stubble bearded rider, off balance and into his two companions, one a dark, swarthy Mexican, the other a redhead.

An oath ripped from the husky man's lips and anger rushed into his eyes. Wade, rocked to his heels, came up against the framing of the doorway. He caught himself, grinned tightly at the rider.

"Sorry," he murmured, and started to move on.

The bearded man lurched forward, threw out a thick arm and checked him. He was not drunk, had consumed only enough of *The Wagonmaster*'s fiery liquor to turn him quarrelsome and belligerent.

"Sorry hell!" he roared. "You think you can go shovin' me around, you got another think comin'!"

He placed himself squarely in front of Luke, huge beefy hands resting on his hips, head thrust forward. His two friends moved out onto the porch and circled softly in until they stood directly behind Wade.

Luke's eyes narrowed and the line of his jaw firmed, began to whiten. Back in the street he could hear the hollow beat of boot heels on the sun baked earth. Beyond the squat puncher, inside the smoky depths of the saloon, chairs scraped as men moved hastily out of the way.

"Said I was sorry," Wade stated in a low, controlled voice. "What do you want from me — my arm?"

"Come on, Del," the redhead said. "Forget it. He never done it a-purpose."

The husky rider hunched lower. He shook his head angrily. Sweat was glistening on his face and his eyes still burned.

"I want you, saddlebum," he said, glaring at Luke. "For maybe ten minutes. Aim to give you a learnin' about pushin' people around."

Anger was beginning to stir within Wade. The collision had been his fault — but it had been accidental and he had apologized. As far as he was concerned it ended there. But if this Del was looking for trouble he had come to the right place. Luke Wade, while never courting such, never ran from it, either.

"Could be a bit of a chore," he said drily, "even with your two swampers helping out."

Del's eyes flamed afresh. "You're mighty tough talkin'!" he snarled. "Now, I'm bettin' that fancy iron you got danglin' off your hip ain't nothin' but show. Pure damn bluff. And I'm bettin' you're the biggest bluff of it all."

"Don't bet on it," Wade replied coldly. "Now, get out of my way. I'm going inside."

"No you ain't — not till I'm done with you!" Del shouted, and lunged, extended hands reaching.

"The hell with it," Luke muttered, and stepped quickly aside. He seized the rider by the shoulders, spun him about. Shoving hard, he sent him stumbling into the arms of his two friends.

"Get him away from me before I have to kill him," he snapped, and turned back to *The Wagonmaster*'s swinging doors.

"Hold on, damn you!" Del screamed. "Else I'll drill you from behind!"

II

Luke Wade froze. He hung there, poised, for several long seconds, and then wheeled slowly. He wanted no trouble, but Del simply wouldn't let it lie. Abruptly, he was all out of patience.

The three men had backed off the porch, now faced him from the street. They had spread out slightly, a yard or so apart. Coolly, Wade considered the disadvantage. Red Hill had fallen silent. He could see several white faces peering through store windows, their features taut and strained. The town marshal had pulled himself erect in the doorway of his office, watched narrowly. Across the way a big, fairly well-dressed man was helping a pretty girl into the buggy in front of *Copp's,* and the thought, *This is going to make me miss talking to him,* passed through Luke's mind. And then he dismissed all vagrant subjects from his consciousness as Del's harsh voice came to him.

"I'm aimin' to see if you can use that there gun you're packin'."

Wade nodded. "Been a few others wonder about it." He glanced toward the town's lawman. The marshal had not moved. Either he did not understand what was happening, or he was unwilling to step in.

Luke's voice was loud in the tense hush. "You stack the odds real good for yourself," he said in a dry voice. He ducked his head at Del's companions. "They cutting a slice of this pie, too?"

"We're bunkies. They'll hang around, make real sure I get a fair shake. We sort of do that — look out for each other."

"I'll bet you do," Wade murmured.

Del laughed. "You gettin' cold feet, mister? Now, I'm a forgivin' man. All you have to do to get out of this is fall right down on your knees and crawl into that saloon. That's all — start crawlin'. . . ."

Luke, his face a mask, kept his eyes fastened to those of Del. "Something I never did do — learn to crawl."

"About time you was learnin'!" the stocky rider yelled, and reached for his pistol.

With the smoothness of an uncoiling spring Luke Wade buckled, swerved to one side. His .45 smashed the silence of the

17

street once, twice before he was prone on the worn boards of *The Wagonmaster's* porch.

Out in the spread of the bright sunshine Del was staggering backward, having great difficulty staying on his feet. Abruptly his pistol fell to the dust. He clutched at his chest with both hands and a slackness settled over his face, displacing the astonishment that had gripped it. He began to sink slowly. Nearby the dark skinned Mexican was on his knees, holding his left side. Blood oozed through his fingers.

Luke Wade saw this from the corner of his eye. His full gaze was on the third man, the redhead, who stared at him through a mixture of fear and amazement. His weapon was no more than half out of its holster. Wade had drawn and fired twice with deadly accuracy before the redhead could even pull his revolver.

"Your turn, Red," Wade called softly through the coiling wisps of smoke.

The puncher released the butt of his pistol, allowed it to drop into place. Fingers spread, he raised his arms slowly.

"Not me," he muttered, shaking his head.

Wade did not stir. "Then get the hell out of here — fast!" he said in savage, biting tone.

Immediately the redhead wheeled to one of the horses at the rack. He swung to the saddle, wheeled about and raced off down the street.

Instantly the town came alive. The marshal started toward the saloon at a fast walk. Men and women came through the doorways of several stores. The rancher, forsaking his daughter, now seated in the buggy, approached in long strides. Voices shouted questions, answers, and somewhere farther along a dog, aroused by the gunshots, barked in a quick, excited way.

Luke drew himself to his feet. He flicked a disdainful glance at the crowd gathering around Del and the Mexican, then, removing his wide brimmed hat, he dusted the front of his worn Levi's and coarse shirt. Men began to pour from the interior of *The Wagonmaster,* crowd by him and add to the considerable assembly already in the street.

"Fastest thing I ever saw!" someone said in an awed voice. "He was through shootin' before any of them even cleared leather."

"Well, he sure didn't miss. Got that Del dead center. And the Mex — he's hurt bad."

"You see that other'n take out? Run like a scared rabbit."

Luke, the hard tension dribbling slowly from his body, turned heavily toward the doorway of the saloon. He needed a drink now worse than ever . . . maybe a couple of them. He took a half step into the broad, murky room, then halted as the marshal's voice caught him.

"Hold up there, you!"

Wearily Wade paused, then turned. He met the old lawman's burning hot gaze.

"Something bothering you, Marshal?"

"Bothering me!" the lawman raged. "You ride into my town, kill one man — maybe two — and then you've got the gall to ask me if something's bothering me! You're damn right there is — you!"

Wade moved his shoulders slightly. "You saw what happened. Was no quarrel on my part. I tried to talk him out of it but he wouldn't listen."

The lawman cocked his head to one side. He was an old man with a white, downcurving moustache. "Was you in his boots, would you? Way it looked to me, you didn't give him no choice."

"He had a choice," Wade cut in coldly. "He could have let it ride if he'd been of a mind. You figure to hold me for it?"

"He can't!" a man at the edge of the porch spoke up indignantly. "We all seen it. If ever a man was crowded into a shootout, it was you. The whole town'll testify to that."

The marshal half turned, gave the speaker a withering glance, then came back to Wade.

"No, reckon there ain't no charges, but I'm serving notice on you now — keep moving. I don't want you around. Hardcase like you draws trouble, and I aim to dodge all of that I can."

Luke grinned wryly. "Man defends himself — and gets tagged a hardcase. Marshal, you got a funny way of figuring things."

"Maybe so, but I ain't standing for no killings in my town."

"You could've stopped it, Henry, if you'd wanted to," a voice broke in from the street. "Don't go passing your problems on to somebody else."

Wade shifted his eyes to the speaker. It was the well dressed rancher with the pretty girl and the buggy. He was a big man with a bluff, firm way about him.

The lawman settled back on his heels, studying the rancher thoughtfully. "Mighty easy for folks to talk, Mr. McMahon, but something like this works both ways. I wasn't so sure it was going to get past the arguing point. And if I'd stepped in then, I'd've had all you folks down my throat for being too strict. You'd've said I was butting in, and was running off the town's business."

"Man wears a star long as you have, Henry, seems you ought to be able to spot the difference between a shootout and an argument," Mr. McMahon snapped. He turned his attention to Wade.

"Who are you, mister?"

"Name's Wade. Luke Wade."

"Just riding through?"

"Maybe. It make a difference?"

"You bet he's riding right through," the lawman said in a hard voice. "I plain won't have him hanging around here, causing trouble —"

The rancher glanced at Luke. "That suit you?"

Wade shrugged. "I'm not looking for trouble, Mr. McMahon. Was just going into the saloon and ask the bartender if he knew where I might find a job for a spell. About out of traveling money."

The rancher's eyes brightened. "You work cattle?"

"Yes, sir. From the Mexican border to Montana. Reckon I know as much as the next man about it."

The old lawman snorted. "Appears to me you know a damn sight more about that hogleg hanging at your side!"

Wade's smile was bleak. "I know about that, too."

"Could be just the man I'm looking for," McMahon said, ignoring the lawman. "If you're meaning that about wanting a job, follow me to my place . . . where's your horse?"

"Around the side," Luke replied. He glanced at the marshal. "All right with you?"

The lawman turned his head and spat in disgust. "Can't see as I got anything to say about it. If he wants to hire you, ain't nothing I can do. But you sure better behave yourself if you come around here again!"

McMahon grinned briefly, the almost pained grimace of a man unaccustomed to displaying levity. "Don't fret over it, Henry. I aim to keep him busy." He nodded to Luke. "You ready to pull out?"

"Soon as I get my sorrel," Wade said, and started across the porch.

He stepped down into the street and headed for the side of the building where, in the shade of a low, spreading cottonwood, he had tied his horse. The words of a man standing with several others near the corner touched him.

"Now what the hell you figure Travis Mc-Mahon wants with a gunslinger?"

Luke Wade paused in stride, then continued on. *Hardcase . . . gunslinger.* He shook his head wryly. For a man trying to mind his own business he had acquired a tough reputation mighty fast in Red Hill!

III

As Luke Wade swung his horse in beside McMahon's buggy he could feel the eyes of the girl, frankly curious, upon him. He turned to meet her gaze, and smiled. She swung her head back around.

She was around twenty, he guessed, with dark hair and eyes. Her skin was a light shade of healthy tan and from what he could tell she had a nicely developed figure that filled the white shirtwaist and skirt outfit she wore to perfection. She was even prettier at close range than he had expected, and he felt his interest brighten.

Women, ordinarily, held only minor attraction for him. Since he was never in one place for over two or three months at a time, most received only passing note from him. But there was something different about this girl, something that had captured his fancy instantly. He wondered who she was . . . McMahon's daughter, he had assumed; he

25

found himself wanting to know for certain.

As if reading his mind, Travis McMahon said, "Wade, like to have you meet my daughter, Samantha. . . . Samantha, this is Luke Wade."

The girl faced him, and nodded. Luke touched the brim of his hat with two fingers. "Pleased to know you, ma'am."

Her eyes sparked. "Don't call me ma'am!" she said stiffly. "I'm younger than you, I expect."

"Likely so, ma'am," Wade replied, some of the grim lines about his mouth softening.

McMahon laughed. "And don't go calling her Sam, either. Riles her something fierce."

She turned again to face him. "I'm happy to meet you," she murmured politely, her words almost lost in the steady *clop-clop* of the trotting horses. "Will you be working for us — for my father?"

Samantha was studying him intently, Luke realized — and realized also that it was a study based on curiosity rather than on personal interest. To her he was a gunfighter, a killer . . . he had just shot down one man, badly wounded another.

"For the Association," McMahon said, answering the question for Wade.

Luke thought he saw a faint twinge of disappointment in her eyes, but he couldn't be sure. He shifted his glance to the rancher.

"Association?"

"A bunch of us ranchers . . . half a dozen or so, scattered up and down the Mangus Valley. We've got ourselves a problem, and after seeing you handle yourself back there in town, taking on those three bully-boys, I figured we could use you."

"Doing what?"

McMahon shifted impatiently on the seat of the buggy, hooked the instep of his boot on the dashboard. "No use me chawing it over twice," he rumbled. "We're having a meeting at my place soon as I get there. You'll learn about it then."

The rancher paused, staring out over the long plains dotted with yellow shaded creosote bush and pumpkin shaped snakeweed. It was poor land, apparently unused by the ranchers. Their spreads would be farther on, beyond the low, black-edged rim of lava rock that lay ahead, Wade guessed.

Abruptly, McMahon said, "Why? You particular about the kind of work you do?"

Wade shifted his shoulders. "Not me — only don't get any wrong ideas about me. I don't make it a habit of gunning men down."

"Way you handled that iron you're wearing, it seemed to come mighty easy."

"Man learns to take care of himself."

There was a long minute of silence, and then the girl, hesitantly, said, "Were — have there been — others?"

"Samantha!" McMahon exclaimed disapprovingly. "You know better than to ask a question like that!" Immediately then he further broke the tacit custom by adding, "Reckon I should have asked you before — are you running from the law?"

Wade said, "No," and let it drop.

It was none of McMahon's business. He intended to keep it on that basis. The law actually was not looking for him, but to say he was unknown to a great number of sheriffs and town marshals would have been untrue. It was a tender subject, best left unexplored.

"Know I've got no right prying into a man's private affairs," the rancher said, his words a deep grumble. "Howsomever, I had to know. Could save us some explaining later."

Wade's glance at the rancher sharpened. "It make a difference if I was wanted by the law?"

McMahon shifted his bulk again on the seat. "Not 'specially, so long as you stand by the Association and don't forget who's paying the bill."

Luke sighed. *Some kind of a range war,* he thought. *A lousy damned range war.* He'd been through one, and when it had been over he'd told himself he'd never get mixed up in another. He began to pull in the sorrel and draw to a halt. Now was the moment to back off — before he ever got in.

McMahon hauled his team to an abrupt stop, glaring at him. "What the hell's the matter?"

"Think maybe you picked the wrong man to hire," Wade answered.

"You said you were looking for a job . . ."

"I am — but I don't aim to get myself tangled up in a war. Did once, and swore I wouldn't again."

"War?" McMahon echoed. "You mean a range war? Who said anything like that?"

Luke frowned. "Just figured that was what you had in mind."

"Well, it ain't," the rancher said bluntly. "Now, supposing you just keep your shirt on until you hear what we've got to offer. Then you can pull out if you've got the notion. Fair enough?"

Luke nodded. "Fair enough," he said, and touched the sorrel with his spurs.

They reached the rim of the *malpais* buttes, and swept down a narrow, gentle slope into a broad valley carpeted with purple tassled grass and dotted with young trees. Far to the left Wade could see the sparkling twist of a river, and beyond it a level horizon of dark faced bluffs. To the right a low range of shadowy, timbered hills formed an opposing barrier. It was beautiful cattle country — ideal, in fact, Luke decided, and in his wanderings across the country he had seen some fine land.

"Thirty miles across and better'n a hundred long," McMahon said in a pride filled voice as he allowed his gaze to roam the lush, green panorama. "Finest cattle raising country in the world. Someday there'll be ranches all over it."

Luke Wade's long standing habit of careful, easy probing came to the fore. McMahon was one of the ranchers that were suspect. He had shown no interest in the killer's gun, but that was no sure indication of innocence.

"Wonder it's not already crowded," he observed. "Not many valleys like this left."

"Only opened up little over three years ago. No water until then."

Luke motioned toward the river. "Looks like plenty."

"Now, yes, but three-four year ago there wasn't any river. Then something happened up north of here. Earthquake, maybe it was. Whole mountain sort of shifted, they say. Next thing you know that river started running. Sure was the making of this part of the territory."

Three or four years ago. . . . Wade was silent while he considered that. "How long you been here?" he asked casually.

"Came in right after the river started flowing. Heard about it from a friend who happened to come through here. Got myself here fast as I could and filed me a claim. Dang good thing I acted pronto. Was a half a dozen others moving in, too."

"How much land have you got?" Luke asked, more to keep the conversation going than anything else while he mulled over the information. That McMahon had been one of those to start ranching just after the murder of Ben Wade and the rustling of their herd was of importance. And soon he would meet several of the others, the members of the Association — all possibilities. A grim satisfaction settled over Luke. He was running in luck for a change.

McMahon's words broke into Wade's thoughts: "What with the free range, I reckon it's close to seventy thousand acres."

Luke had to connect the statement with the question he had asked — and almost forgotten. He nodded. "Man could fatten a lot of steers on that much grass. How big a herd you running?"

McMahon looked down. "Going to surprise you, maybe, but all I've got is a hundred and fifty head or so. Same with all the others. We're all small, just getting started. None of us got enough stock to brag about — and we're all plenty shy of cash, mostly because of what happened last year."

"What was that?" Wade asked, angling the sorrel in closer to the buggy in order to hear better.

"You'll get the story at the meeting," the rancher said. He pointed to a small cluster of buildings grouped in the center of small cottonwoods that appeared suddenly on their left. A flat faced butte lay to the south end: it had hidden the ranch from view until they were almost upon it.

"That's my place. Ain't much yet, but if things'll go right it will be someday. . . . Looks like the rest of the boys are already there. Reckon we better hurry it up a mite and get the meeting started."

Luke Wade touched the sorrel with his rowels as McMahon shook his team into a gallop. He was anxious, too; he wanted a good look at all the men of the Association

— men who had moved into the Mangus Valley country around three years ago.

IV

An older edition of Samantha McMahon stood in the doorway of the ranchhouse as they wheeled into the yard. Seven of eight men, all wearing the hard finished garb of working ranchers, lounged in the shade of the wagonshed. McMahon, pausing long enough to allow his daughter to collect her parcels and dismount, moved on toward them.

Wade, a quietness possessing him at the thought that he might, at last, be coming face to face with the ruthless killer he had sought for so long, guided the sorrel to one of the pole corrals and swung down. Winding the leathers around one of the cross legs, he walked slowly to where McMahon and the others had gathered. The big rancher, out of his buggy, was speaking hurriedly and earnestly to the men. Evidently he was giving them an account of what had happened in Red Hill.

As Luke moved up the group parted, spread out to meet him. Most were smiling but there were a couple who regarded him soberly, almost with hostility.

"Just been telling the boys about your trouble in town," McMahon rumbled. "And how you handled yourself."

Wade merely waited, saying nothing. He reached into his shirt pocket, produced the makings, and began a cigarette. Face tipped down, he gave each rancher close, hard scrutiny. Any one of them could be his man.

"Reckon first thing we ought to do is make some introductions," McMahon said, leaning back against the hind wheel of a light wagon. He waved a hand at a graying, long faced man. "This here's Charlie Peck, Luke. Owns the place west of mine."

Peck stepped forward. Wade watched his eyes intently. The rancher said, "Pleased to meet you," and shook hands.

A tall, smiling man with lean, somewhat sharp features stood next to Peck. Not waiting for McMahon, he thrust out his arm, grasped Luke's hand in a firm grip.

"I'm Helm Stokes. . . . It's a pleasure. From what Travis told us you must've made the town set up and take notice."

Wade smiled with his eyes, liking the rancher immediately. McMahon motioned to a third man. "Otis Kline."

Kline ducked his head forward. He was one of the older ones, around fifty, Luke guessed, a husky, square faced sort of individual. He did not offer his hand.

"How do," he said, then added, "Ain't so sure it's not a mistake, bringing you here. I don't hold with killing."

"Neither do I," Luke replied coolly. "Man does what he has to sometimes."

"There's other ways," Kline said.

From behind the ranch a boy, somewhere in his late teens, pushed forward, reached for Luke's hand. He was smiling broadly, plainly pleased to meet Wade.

"I'm Joe Dee Kline," he said. "You sure must be a wonder with that fancy gun you're packin'."

The squat rancher's son, Luke supposed, and started to say something, but Mc-Mahon cut in on his intentions.

"Albert Dunn. Owns the Square D layout."

Dunn, like Peck, was older. He had a round face, and he showed evidences of once having been considerably heavier, but age and the dry, hard labor of ranch life had trimmed him down.

"A pleasure," the rancher said, and inclined his head.

"Will Johnson," McMahon continued, pointing to a slightly built, balding man. "And the last one there, with the mashed-in nose, is Hank Timmons. Hank lost an argument with a bronc he was bustin'."

Both greeted Wade, and stepped back into the line. Luke, saying nothing, swept the ranchers with his intent glance once again. None had revealed any reaction to the gun he carried — none except Joe Dee Kline, and his was one of boyish admiration. And all, excluding the boy, of course, and possibly Johnson, fit the vague description of the killer left him by his father — particularly Travis McMahon, he realized with a start. The scar would be the only sure proof.

"We're getting together to talk about the drive we're starting tomorrow," McMahon said, looking directly at Luke. "But first I reckon we ought to fill you in some." He shifted his eyes to Stokes. "You lay it out for him, Helm."

Stokes squatted on his heels and drew a cigar from his pocket. He bit off the end, spat, and struck a match to the tip. He exhaled a cloud of blue smoke, considered it briefly, then began to speak.

"We've got us a little different sort of a problem up here in Mangus Valley. We're all new and just getting started. Means we ain't big enough to do things on our own so we all have to work together.

"And none of us has much stock, so what we have to do is pool what we want to sell and make a drive to the railhead. Town called Anson's Fork. East of here. Takes about five days to make the drive."

Luke vaguely recalled the settlement. He had passed through it once, perhaps twice in the course of his wandering. About all he could remember about it was the name itself. All towns eventually got to where they looked alike.

"Herd generally tots up to a couple hundred head. Not big, as herds go, but every steer means plenty to the man who owns him."

"Means the difference in making a go of our places, or winding up broke — if we lose them this time," Charlie Peck said.

"Losing them?" Wade said, his brows lifting.

Stokes nodded. "This'll be the third time we've made the drive. First year we got them through. Last year we wasn't so lucky."

The rancher paused, and scratched at the ground with a twig. Apparently what had happened that previous summer was a painful memory. Luke waited.

"Last year," McMahon finished in a savage, angry tone, "the goddam rustlers hit us — got away with the whole herd!"

"About ruined me," Otis Kline said, wagging his head dolefully. "Forty of them critters was mine — and they was worth sixteen dollars apiece. I was figuring strong on that cash. Had it in mind to do a right smart amount of fixing up around my place. Way it turned out, me and my family lived on beans and cornbread all winter."

"If it happens again," Albert Dunn murmured, "I'm through. I'm pulling out."

Wade's voice was incredulous. "You never found any trace of the herd? How could a couple hundred steers just drop out of sight?"

"Sounds plumb loco," Stokes agreed, "but that's the way it was. I ramrodded the drive, so I was there. You got to remember this: we didn't have any regular drovers. Was just me, one of my hired hands and another fellow — rancher named Willson. He got killed by the rustlers.

"They jumped us about dark third day out. Some rough country between here and the railhead — brushy canyons and the like. Willson stopped a bullet while he was building a fire for night camp. My man was out tending the herd and they knocked him over the head, tied him up and left him laying in the mesquite."

Stokes hesitated again, once more toying with the twig. His face was stiff, solemn.

"Helm tried to stop the rustlers by himself," McMahon said, taking up the account. "But they drove him back to some buttes and pinned him down with rifles. They kept him there for better'n a day. They'd have killed him sure, I reckon, if he'd showed his head."

Luke still found it hard to understand. "But two hundred steers — there'd be dust, tracks. Seems like a man could've followed, even a couple of days later."

"Grass country," Stokes said. "Not much dust. On top of that, it rained. First thing I did when I saw that the pair pinning me down had pulled out — that was a day and a night later — was to try and locate the stock. It was too late then."

"What about the railhead? Anybody ever show up there with your beef?"

"Never did. Oh, several herds came in, but they were from other ranches east and north of here. None of our stuff was ever seen."

For several moments Luke was silent; then he said, "Looks like the answer is for all of you to take a hand in the drive. Give yourself more protection."

"Sounds simple," McMahon agreed, "only it ain't. Ranching's a family affair with each one of us. I mean, we do our own work. None of us ever has enough ready cash to hire help, which means we have to stay pretty close to home. Only reason Stokes can get away is that he ain't married. He's not trying to do so much — like the rest of us."

"Main reason I volunteered to boss the drive," Stokes said. "Don't have but mighty little to lose. I can afford to take the time off. Rest of the ranchers, well, if they ain't home the work just don't get done — and this is a mighty important time of the year around here."

Luke Wade understood the problem. It was the same everywhere. Building a ranch was a hard, grubbing life in the beginning. A man depended upon his wife and children for help in many ways, and got it; but the major portion of the work was of a nature that only he could handle.

And he was realizing, too, the importance of a successful drive to them. Each gambled what stock he figured he could afford to sell for the sake of cash money. If the sale were completed the family, and the ranch, could make it through the winter months fairly well. If the stock were lost, it was a hard, bitter blow that could shut a man down, end his hopes and dreams.

But he had his own problems, he reminded himself suddenly. He couldn't afford to get too involved — only to the point of what it meant in terms of money to him.

"Where do I fit?" he asked then.

"You'll ride guard," McMahon said promptly. "Like a shotgun man on a stage. Only you'll be watching out for rustlers. Seeing you back there in town give me the idea. Stokes has agreed to boss the drive again. He'll take along one of his hands, and Kline's boy, Joe Dee, wants to go. Makes three to handle the herd. Not enough, I know, but it's the best we can do."

"With you along doing the outriding and keeping your eyes peeled," Stokes said, "I figure three'll be all we need. We'll be able to sort of bear down on the herd, keep it moving good."

A trail guard . . . outrider for a bunch of cows. He'd had worse jobs — besides, it could put him one step closer to the man who'd murdered Ben Wade. "What's the pay?" he asked.

"Talked it over," McMahon said. "We're willing to pay you four bits a head for every steer that's tallied into the loading pens at the railhead. Figures up to a hundred dollars, more or less — for about a week's work."

"But only if you get through," Dunn warned. "If we don't make a sale I couldn't scrape up enough cash to buy you a square meal."

"Me neither," Peck added.

There was silence after that. It would be good pay, Luke realized, real good. More than he could make in three months at a regular ranch job. But worth more than all were the personal advantages that had already occurred to him. He could be getting close to his father's killer.

"You've got yourself a deal," he said.

McMahon smiled broadly. "Fine, fine. Glad it's all settled. Now, let's go up to the house. Expect the missus has got some coffee ready for us."

V

Mrs. McMahon, aided by Samantha, now in a simple gingham print, had coffee and a small wedge of dried apple pie laid out in neat rows on the kitchen table when the men entered the low ceilinged house.

Each helped himself, and then found a place in the front room or back porch to enjoy the light repast. The coffee was good, the pie excellent and Luke Wade found himself hoping there might be seconds, but he would ask for none. From what he had heard in the wagonshed all of the Mangus Valley ranchers were on a shoestring footing and it wouldn't be right to take advantage of their hospitality.

He looked up after finishing off the pie and discovered Mrs. McMahon watching him from across the kitchen. Samantha favored her entirely and it was as though he were glancing at the girl twenty years from that moment.

Luke nodded politely. "It was fine pie, ma'am. I enjoyed it."

She gave him a restrained smile, and said, "We haven't been introduced, but I guess you are Mr. Wade."

"Yes'm . . . Luke Wade," he replied. "I —"

McMahon, overhearing partly, wheeled. "Oh, Molly, I forgot to —"

"We've just met," she said, a faint thread of disapproval in her tone. "He enjoyed my pie."

"Man'd be crazy if he didn't," the rancher declared. "Luke's going to work for the Association — leastwise long enough to see the herd through to the railhead."

Mrs. McMahon nodded. "I'm sure there'll be no trouble, then — not after what Samantha told me."

Something akin to anger stirred within Luke Wade. Molly McMahon disliked him, that was plain, and she was basing her opinions of him on the shootout at Red Hill. He started to say something, to explain and make her understand that he didn't while away his time shooting men to death — and then thought better of it.

The effort wasn't worth the end result — and it would be smart not to get too friendly with any of the ranchers and their families. It could complicate matters later.

"How about more coffee?" McMahon asked, trying to cover his wife's hostility.

Luke began a refusal, but hushed when the rancher refilled his cup unheedingly. When it was full he said, "Obliged to you," and walked out onto the rear porch slowly. Molly McMahon said something in a sharp tone to her husband but Wade gave it no attention, preferring not to hear.

The remainder of the ranchers were scattered throughout the house, conversing in pairs and groups. Luke wondered what had become of Samantha. He hadn't noticed her for some time.

He halted on the porch, grateful for the faint breeze blowing in from the plains. On ahead, beyond McMahon's barn and lesser sheds, he could see a garden, green with half grown stalks of corn, squat tomato plants, peppers and other vegetables. All appeared to be thriving.

A small orchard had been planted, but the trees were yet too young to bear. Another couple of years, at least, Luke estimated. There was a fenced-in chicken yard where a dozen or more hens and a solitary rooster scuffled in the dust, and in the shade on the north side of the barn a cow munched contentedly on her cud.

Travis McMahon had a fine start — but it

was easy to see the rancher trod a thin line. The slightest thing going wrong could mean disaster. And it would be the same with all the others in Mangus Valley . . . all but Helm Stokes, perhaps. He struck Luke as being a man who didn't particularly care whether the sun rose or not. Being unmarried made him that way, likely; he could weather adversity without feeling its brutal pinch.

At that moment Samantha, accompanied by Joe Dee Kline, emerged from the barn. Unaccountably, Luke felt a slight twinge of resentment at seeing them together — and then he grinned wryly. What the hell was wrong with him? What right had he to have feelings of any sort about the girl? Anyway, Joe Dee was several years younger than she was.

He watched them approach the house, Samantha easy and graceful in her walk, the boy hovering anxiously nearby and talking rapidly. She made a fetching picture in the bright sunlight, her dark hair glinting, her skin soft and creamy looking.

They reached the porch, entered and halted before Luke. At once Joe Dee said, "Mr. Wade's going with us on the drive tomorrow."

"Call me Luke," Wade said, feeling uncommonly old before the boy's enthusiasm.

"He's going with us," the boy repeated. "Be the guard. We'll get the herd through this time sure!"

Samantha studied Wade soberly. "I'm sure you will."

"Nobody'll try jumpin' us — not with him along. You can bet on that."

"Mr. Wade's reputation should guarantee it," she said dryly.

From the interior of the house Otis Kline's deep voice sounded: "Joe Dee! Let's get started. Lot of work to be done around the place before you leave."

"Yes, pa," the boy answered. He grinned slyly at the girl. "So long, Sam . . . see you when I get back."

She frowned, then made a face at him. "Good-bye, Joe Dee. Take care."

"You bet," the boy said, then, grinning at Luke, added, "See you in the morning, Mr. Wade."

Luke watched him turn and enter the kitchen, and hurry on into the adjoining parlor. Others were leaving and he wondered, briefly, if he should hunt up Stokes and arrange to stay the night with him at his place so as to be on hand the following morning. He decided to let matters take their course. If Stokes wanted him, he'd sing out. Besides, it was pleasant being there with Samantha.

"I was showing Joe Dee our new colt," she said, the stiffness gone from her tone. "Foaled about a week ago. A real pretty little bay with four white stockings. Would you like to see him?"

Wade smiled. "You bet I would," he said, placing his empty cap on a closeby shelf. "Always had a weakness for bays."

"So you ride a sorrel," she said mischievously.

"Just happens so," he said quietly, following her out into the yard. "Still like bays."

She half turned, and stared at him intently. "You mean that, don't you? I'm sorry; I didn't intend to josh you about it."

"Forget it," he said, feeling awkward about his actions.

Samantha continued to study him. "I guess it's what you are that makes you so dead serious — so withdrawn, sort of. . . ."

"What I am? What's that?"

She shrugged her slight shoulders. "A gunman," she said frankly. "It makes you the way you are."

He laughed. "I'm no hired killer, if that's what you're thinking. I never shot it out with a man in my life unless I was forced into it . . . just like this morning. Expect every man goes through the same experience a few times in his life. Some back off and run away, and others stand their ground. I just happen to be one that doesn't believe in walking away."

Samantha was quiet for a time. Over in the orchard a meadowlark whistled cheerfully. She glanced in that direction, then said, "I think I know what you mean. But it isn't that — it's something else that makes you the sort you are. . . . What is it?"

Wade's jaw hardened. He was vaguely irritated and somewhat surprised by the girl's perception. He forced a smile, pointed at the open doorway leading into the barn immediately ahead.

"That where you've got the colt?"

She nodded, crossed in front of him and led the way to one of the stalls arranged along the wall of the bulky structure. She halted, still not speaking.

A leggy colt, sleek and shining in the murky light, turned a narrow head to view them, then resumed his nuzzling of the mare beside him.

"A real fine bit of horseflesh," Luke said. "Going to make a good animal."

"You don't care to talk about it?" Samantha said.

He stood silent, momentarily put to a loss

by the question. Then he realized she was still on the same subject.

"No," he said gruffly. "I don't care to talk about it."

Maybe he should . . . maybe he should ask her about her father, start out by inquiring as to whether he'd been in the war or not, gradually lead up to the scar — and if he had one. If so, where? And ask about the others — Stokes, Kline, Charlie Peck . . . all of them. They were all prospects for the business end of his killer's gun. Why not involve her in it, too?

Somehow he could not . . . not right then, anyway. Maybe later, after the drive, when they were better acquainted. It just wasn't the proper moment. . . . Vaguely, he wondered why he should feel that way. Never before had he permitted anything or anybody to hinder the quest — why now? Maybe he really didn't want to know; maybe he was afraid of the answers he would get from her. . . . He pulled himself up short. That was crazy thinking. He'd find out soon enough, and if it turned out to be Travis McMahon he wanted — well, so be it.

"I'm sorry," he heard her say as she turned toward the door. "Whatever it is, it must trouble you a lot."

He fell in behind her. "Didn't know it

showed that much. But don't worry about it. I've lived with it a long time."

He halted, aware of someone standing in the doorway. It was McMahon, his face stiff, almost angry. Beyond him, her expression dark as a thundercloud, Molly McMahon watched from the porch.

"I was showing Luke — Mr. Wade the colt," Samantha said.

The rancher's eyes were sharp. "Your ma wants you, Samantha."

The girl sobered at his tone, gave him a disturbed look and hurried out into the yard. McMahon jerked his thumb toward Luke's sorrel.

"Expect you'd better line out for Stoke's place," he said. "You'll be spending the night with him."

It was evident from the rancher's manner that plans had been changed. Likely McMahon had intended for him to stay the night under his roof and then join Stokes and the others in the morning. Something had altered that — something that had to do with Samantha, he guessed. Probably the McMahons didn't relish the idea of their daughter getting too friendly with a gunslinger.

Wade sighed inwardly, and brushed aside the impatience that moved through him.

Just as well. . . . He recalled his previous determination not to get involved with any of the Mangus Valley people. And he guessed he couldn't blame the McMahons. Likely he would feel the same if he had a daughter.

"Whatever you say," he murmured. "How do I find Stokes?"

McMahon backed into the yard, pointed into the northwest. He settled his finger upon a triangular peak near the end of a distant mountain.

"Ride straight for that . . . the Stokes place lays about a third of the way. Can't miss it."

Wade nodded his thanks, and struck out across the hard-pack for the sorrel. He heard the rancher say, "Good luck," but he did not turn to voice a reply, simply lifted his hand and allowed it to fall.

Mounting, he wheeled about. Abreast of the house, he glanced toward the porch. Samantha had disappeared inside. Molly McMahon stood there, her expression of disapproval still holding. He touched the brim of his hat and continued on.

When he rode out of the yard moments later he could still feel her gaze; it seemed to be pushing him, driving him as though she were determined to remove him from her family circle and life as quickly as possible.

It was just as well, he told himself again.

VI

Luke Wade took his time reaching the Stokes ranch. He circled wide, noting the fine rangeland across which he rode, enjoying occasional glimpses of blue quail, long eared jackrabbits and swift winged doves. He paused once, enraptured by the sight of a great, golden eagle soaring high overhead. He watched, breathless, as the huge bird abruptly plummeted earthward, seized some luckless small animal in its talons, and rushed away.

Apparently it had been a wet spring. Flowers splashed their color at every hand: clumps of goldenrod, patches of verbenas, blankets of fleabane and yellow hearted asters, and entire slopes of red bee plant.

He rode into the Stokes yard shortly after full dark. It was a much smaller ranch, insofar as structures went, than McMahon's. There appeared to be only the main house, a closeby combination kitchen and bunkhouse, a privy and a few small sheds, besides the corrals. There were cattle inside the enclosures. They constituted the herd, he assumed, that was to be driven to the railhead.

The main house was in darkness but a light glowed through the kitchen window, and after stabling the sorrel and throwing down a quantity of feed for him Luke made his way to that structure.

The cook, a gangling, elderly man in tattered overalls, glanced up sourly as he entered. The room was miserably hot, filled with the odor of fresh bread and frying meat. A platter stacked high with beef already cooked sat in the center of a wide table, along with several loaves of cooling bread. The man was preparing sandwiches for the drive.

"Who might you be?" he demanded, peering through bushy, gray brows.

"Wade. Grub sure smells good."

"Wade, eh? Stokes said you was stayin' the night with the McMahons. Didn't fix you no meal."

"Plans got changed. Don't go to any bother. A piece of that meat and some bread will do me. And coffee, if there's any left."

The cook shrugged and resumed his

chore. "Help yourself. Cup there on the shelf."

Luke, after selecting some of the beef and bread and pouring himself a cup of the strong coffee, sat down at the table. He ate slowly, relishing the savory food.

"You'll be carryin' your own grub," the old man said. "Stokes ain't takin' no chuck wagon. Says there ain't enough men goin' for that."

"Expect he's right. Man won't have much time to eat anyway. . . . You know my name. Like to know yours."

"Friends call me Caleb. . . . Likely wastin' my time fixin' all these sandwiches, but if I don't there'll be a lot of belly-achin'."

"I'll eat mine," Luke said. "Bread's sure just right. So's the meat."

Caleb looked up, clearly pleased. "Find yourself some fresh butter over there in the window box. Makes that bread some tastier."

Luke immediately helped himself to another thick slice of the bread, this time fortifying it with a large chunk of butter.

"You're welcome to come do my cookin' anytime you want," he said, resuming his chair.

Caleb grinned a toothy appreciation.

"Obliged to you, but I reckon I'm set for a spell."

"How long you been with Stokes?"

"A month, maybe two."

"You acquainted with this part of the country?"

The old cook continued to work with his sandwiches. "Been around, off and on, ten, twelve year."

Luke allowed that to ride. Unconsciously, he had slipped into the old pattern of probing that had become second nature with him.

"This Stokes seems a right nice fellow. Only met him today. You know him long?"

"Not long."

"Hear he's been here about three years."

"Reckon so."

"Figure I'm going to like working with him. Was he in the war?"

Caleb laid down his knife. He cast a sideward glance at the window. "Must've been that there dang butter," he muttered.

"Butter? What about it?"

"Makin' you fire all them questions at me — which I ain't answerin'."

Luke grinned. He'd been trapped before and he'd learned the best way out was to laugh it off.

"Sure, old timer . . . was just wanting to

know the man better."

"Well," Caleb drawled, "I don't know nothin' about Stokes and I reckon if you're goin' to learn anything, best you ask him yourself."

"Just what I'll do," Luke said, rising. "Obliged to you for the meal. Was plenty good. Any idea where I can bed down?"

"Right through that there door," Caleb said, pointing with the knife to the wall behind Luke. "You'll find a bunk that ain't bein' slept in. Crawl right in."

"Rest of the boys already turned in?"

"Yeh . . . Pete and Al Cobb and Jim Leggett. They're in there."

"That Stokes' whole crew?"

"Yep. That's all of them."

"Which one's going on the drive?"

Caleb sighed, dropped his knife onto the table. "Jim Leggett, so I hear. Stokes is leavin' the others and me to look after the place while he's gone. Why, I sure don't know. Ain't nothin' worth lookin' after. Now, dang it — you wantin' to know anything else?"

Wade grinned, and said, "No . . . guess you've said it all. Good night."

" 'Night," Caleb replied, and recovered his knife. "Don't be forgettin' your sack of vittles when you pull out, come mornin'. Be here on the table."

"I won't," Luke said, and, opening the door, he turned into the pitch dark, stuffy interior of the bunkroom.

VII

Helm Stokes was in the kitchen drinking black coffee when Wade entered shortly after four o'clock that next morning. The big rancher gave Luke a broad smile and offered his hand.

"Glad to see you, Wade. Sorry I wasn't up when you rode in last night."

"It's all right," Luke replied. "Caleb here took care of me fine. About ready to head out?"

"Soon as you can get some breakfast down. Leggett and the others are already shaping up the herd."

The cook set a plate of meat and potatoes before Luke and filled a tin cup to the brim with steaming coffee for him. Wade sat down and began to eat.

"You said something about your men getting the herd underway. You decide to take your whole crew?" he asked.

Stokes shook his head. "Only Leggett. Al

and Pete will stay with us long enough to get things started." The rancher paused, glanced through the window at the sky. "Going to be another scorcher."

"Here's your vittles," Caleb broke in, pushing a bulging, string tied flour sack across the table at Luke. "Don't go trottin' off without 'em."

Luke smiled, and thanked the old man. They were still friends, he guessed. He finished his plate and rose, taking the provisions with him. Stokes was still looking out through the streaky glass of the window.

"Guess I'm ready — soon as I get my horse," Luke said.

Stokes wheeled, then hurriedly drained his cup. "Fine. Meet you outside."

The rancher, astride a tall, black gelding, was waiting when Luke swung into the yard. He pointed to a shifting, irregular mass on the mesa a quarter mile distant.

"Looks like the boys have got them moving."

They rode off the hard-pack onto the grassy plain and angled toward the moving herd. A faint film of dust was rising, now hung like a transparent, dark edged cloud against the gray flare of coming daylight. In only a few minutes they had caught up with the cattle.

Wade, having had his time with trail drives, gave the herd quick appraisal. It was ragged, and far from being properly shaped-up. But he guessed he was too critical; the drive was just getting underway. Give it another hour or so and matters should improve.

He could see young Joe Dee Kline riding swing, at their left, but as near as he could tell no one was at point yet, leading the cattle. Three riders loomed up in the half light to his right and loped toward Stokes. From habit, Luke eyed them speculatively.

"Got 'em movin'," a thin, balding man said, wiping at his face.

Stokes nodded. He waved a hand at Wade. "This here's Luke Wade, boys. He's the man that done all the hell-fire shooting in town yesterday. Hired him on to ride guard for us. . . . Luke, baldy there is Jim Leggett. Other two work for me. Al Cobb's the one on the buckskin . . . Pete Nogal's the one with the fancy saddle."

The three riders nodded unsmilingly. All were quiet faced men, almost secretive. Luke acknowledged the introductions with a faint tip of his head.

Stokes said, "Al, you and Pete might as well drop back. We can handle it from here."

Immediately the two men whirled away

and struck out at a lope for the ranchhouse. Stokes raised himself in his stirrups and considered the herd. After a few moments he turned to Leggett.

"Jim, you and the boy'll have to ride swing and look after the stragglers, too. Just keep whipping back and forth. I'll take the point." He paused, glancing at Luke. "You do what you figure best. I'd suggest you move out front, keep ahead of us. Watch better from there."

Wade said, "That's what I had in mind. Want me to tell the boy when I go by?"

"Obliged to you if you would."

Luke spurred off, circled the loosely formed herd, beginning now to string out far too thin, and galloped toward Joe Dee. The boy saw him coming, and drew to a halt. He grinned broadly through the dust and sweat already streaking his face.

"Mornin', Mr. Wade!"

"Morning, Joe Dee," Luke answered. "Stokes says you're to work this side, and keep after the stragglers. Leggett's doing the same on the right."

"Sure," the boy said agreeably. He twisted about and looked to the rear. "Looks like I got me some stragglers right now. See you later!"

Joe Dee raced off and Luke continued on,

forging out ahead of the cattle. Cresting a low hill, he studied the herd once more: if Stokes didn't hurry up and get the steers bunched, a hard day would lie ahead for the horses and their riders.

But that was the rancher's problem. He had his own job to look out for. Removing his hat, he mopped at the sweat accumulation; as Stokes had observed, it was going to be hot. Good thing the cattle had watered before the drive had begun.

They were moving across a broad, grassy swale that lifted slightly toward the Sacramento Mountains to the east. The going would not be so easy once they reached the hills, Wade knew. And his own job would be more difficult. He would have to be doubly alert, for the wild canyons studded with rock and thick underbrush would be ideal for rustlers to lay their ambush.

Stokes would have his hands full, too, getting the herd through, and Luke didn't envy him the task. With only two drovers, inexperienced ones at that, he would be fortunate to make it without loss.

Again Luke brushed that worry aside; moving the stock was Helm Stokes' chore — his was to keep the rustlers at bay if any materialized along the trail. But deep inside he held a hope that the herd would make it through — and he was determined to uphold his bargain to that end. At first it had been only the money he would receive, and the opportunities to know better the ranchers of Mangus Valley, that had interested him; now another factor concerned him — if the drive failed as it had that previous year, all these ranchers would face a bleak future and possibly complete ruin.

That should have no meaning for him, he told himself as the sorrel plodded slowly on, keeping pace with the flowing sea of brown, white and tan now below. He should hold to his purpose — and so far he had accomplished little in determining which, if any, of the Mangus Valley ranchers was the man he sought.

The need for a job had got in the way — the necessity for hard cash. If it hadn't been for that he could, at that moment, have been prowling about, making inquiries and coming up, possibly, with helpful information. But everything had been sidetracked, and he was losing time.

He was overlooking Helm Stokes . . . and Joe Dee Kline. While neither seemed likely to be the killer, they might be able to give him some ideas. When they bedded the herd at sundown and were all together again, he'd drop a few casual questions. He should take advantage of every moment.

The day wore on, hot and windy. By mid-afternoon both man and beast were suffering under the lash of the sun. Stokes had brought no extra horses, an indication of inexperience to Wade, and Luke knew trouble would face them the following day when they'd reach the rugged, sprawling Sacramentos.

They made an early night camp and Stokes upset Luke's plans by separating the riders, Luke included, and stationing them on the four sides of the herd. It was a wise precaution and Wade approved — but it did prevent his making the inquiries he had in mind.

They were on the move again by five o'clock the next morning, and three hours later were entering the mountains through the narrow mouth of a steep walled canyon.

The heat, trapped by the rock walls, shielded from any breeze, was monstrous, equal almost to that of the blazing deserts of northern Mexico and lower Arizona. The horses tired quickly and the herd became unruly, started to break up, stall and refuse to continue. Stokes, aided by young Kline and Jim Leggett, rushed ceaselessly back and forth through the milling animals, shouting, cursing, lashing the brutes with folded ropes. Several times Helm Stokes fired his pistol as he tried to regain control of the stubborn cattle.

Their efforts met with little success, and Luke, watching impatiently from a ledge a hundred feet or so above the trail, saw that disaster was imminent unless something were done fast.

He made a final sweep of the area with his glance, saw no horsemen that might be a threat, and rode down to give the cattleman a hand. The herd was in confusion; steers were plunging erratically off into the maze of rock and brush, bawling loudly. Some stood motionless, legs spraddled, refusing to move; others had turned about and were bucking the flow, trying to double back up the canyon. As he wheeled in beside Stokes, the rancher, his face caked with dust and sweat, flung him an exasperated look.

"For hell's sake quit fighting them!" Luke yelled above the tumult as he shook out his rope. "Let 'em go!"

"Heat's turned them loco!" the rancher shouted.

"I can see that — but they can't go anywhere but on down canyon, or back. Walls are too steep for them to climb. You keep this up and you're going to lose some stock!"

An old, gray mossy-horn whirled suddenly, cut away from the others of his kind, and came charging straight for the two men. Instantly Wade spurred the sorrel forward, lash swinging from his hand. When only paces separated him from the heat-maddened steer, he swerved sharp left, brought the rope down with stinging force across the brute's bulging eyes and nose.

The steer bawled, veered right, and once again was moving with the herd. Wade cut back to where Stokes was fighting his horse, trying to keep him crowding the rumps of a small jag of stock.

"Like I said," Luke resumed, "they can't go nowhere but back or on. Let 'em scatter — sides of the canyon will stop them. All we got to do is trail behind and see that none of them double back."

Stokes nodded his head in understanding. He brushed at his face and said, "I'll hail in Leggett and the boy. With the four of us riding abreast, like you say, we ought to get them down the canyon."

Luke watched him move ahead into the boiling dust cloud and disappear. A small knot of steers off to his left began to balk, stall and try to turn about. Lifting his rope, Luke forced the sorrel in close, and hammered at the stubborn animals until they broke and moved on.

Stokes, with Leggett and Joe Dee, hove into view. The rancher was waving his arms, yelling his instructions above the noise of the herd. Luke joined them and together they dropped back and took up trailing positions across the floor of the canyon. Pushing steadily, they kept the herd moving in front of them. It was a dry, choking task that lasted almost until sundown, but finally the ragged, narrow slash in the mountains opened up and the herd spilled slowly out onto a broad saddle.

"River anywhere close?" Wade asked, curving in near to the rancher. With the thirst the cattle would have after the canyon's passage, there would be no holding them if they got wind of water.

Stokes shook his head. "Not until tomorrow. Almost a full day from here."

"Expect they'll settle down then. They're plenty tired."

The rancher nodded, and said, "That goes for all of us — and the horses, too. Glad you come up with that idea of pushing them through. We'd be back there yet if you hadn't."

Wade said nothing. It had been no act of brilliance on his part — simply common trail driving sense born of experience. He liked Helm Stokes as a man, but when they returned to Mangus Valley he was going to tell Travis McMahon that the ranchers would be smart to hire a professional trail herd boss the next time they planned a drive; it could prove cheaper in the long run. They were lucky there weren't a dozen or more dead and crippled steers back up in the rocks.

"You making camp on the flat?" he asked, looking up to the extreme tip of a rocky ledge a half mile to his left.

Stokes glanced at the herd moving slowly out onto the grassy plain. "Looks like a good spot."

Wade said, "For a fact. Think I'll have a look from that point over there, see if we've got any company. Meet you at camp."

"We'll have coffee boiling," the rancher said, and moved on.

Luke swung back across the saddle, tired but glad that the emergency was over. He reached the first rocky outcropping below the ledge and urged the worn sorrel up the steep trail. Coming to the shelf, he halted and dismounted. Leaving his horse, he crawled out to the point and pulled himself upright.

Seemingly far below he could see the herd trickling lazily into the center of the grassy

71

hollow. His eyes picked up Kline and Leggett, cutting back toward Stokes, evidently seeking the rancher out to get further orders. Stokes apparently was somewhere in the line of brush to their left. Luke could not locate him.

He could see no one else on the broad plain, and turning back, he searched the rough slopes of the hills through which they had just passed. There were only the twisted shapes of the pinons and cedars, the stiff pines, the shadowy rocks now beginning to cool.

"So far so good," he murmured aloud and took a half step toward the edge of the shelf below which the sorrel waited.

At that exact instant a powerful force slapped against his head. It spun him half about as a shower of lights, accompanied by the hollow, flat sound of a gunshot, burst before his eyes.

He tried to collect his flagging wits, then staggered again as a second, shocking wallop rocked him and sent raging pain searing through his breast. He felt his knees buckle and more pain surged through him in an overpowering wave. And then all was darkness.

VIII

Luke Wade opened his eyes with considerable effort. At first everything was a gray, ragged blur and sickening pain hammered relentlessly at his head. He lay quietly and the blur gradually faded.

He was flat on his back on a ledge. A sharp cornered stone was digging into his left kidney, but the pain it engendered in no way matched that in his head and left shoulder when he tried to move, so he simply endured it.

The low, velvet black of the star-studded sky was over him and the light from a quarter moon was pale, scarcely illuminating the cold surface of the ledge. He had been shot, he now realized. Twice. And he had to do something about it, or he would bleed to death.

He stirred again, trying to sit up. The slogging pain paralyzed his muscles and he had no strength at all. He did succeed, finally, in squirming off the cruel edge of the rock.

He knew he had to rouse himself, shake off the deadly lethargy — do something about his wounds. He'd sure as hell bleed to death, he warned himself again. Mustering his strength, he tried to rise. Abruptly he was violently sick and retched deeply — and then everything became gray once more and he sank back.

It was cold . . . Wade became aware of that. His lids fluttered open. Night was still upon him, and the moon had moved considerably since he'd last seen it. But the terrible pain in his head and the throbbing in his shoulder and breast had not changed; they were as agonizing as before.

He thought again of his wounds and the necessity for doing something about them. He had already lost too much blood, and it was continuing to seep steadily from his body. He fought himself to a sitting position. Wave upon wave of nausea swept over him and he vomited uncontrollably. Finally that ceased, and he sat head down, shoulders slumped. He had no strength remaining — but at least he was still upright.

After a time he stirred. Gingerly, he explored that portion of his throbbing head where he could feel a stinging sensation. His fingers encountered sticky moisture —

a line of it that extended from a point above his temple to the back of his head. He managed a tight grin. The bullet had grazed him . . . close. . . . A fraction of an inch more and he would have known nothing about it.

He slumped again, exhausted by his slight efforts. Minutes later he began to probe the wound in his shoulder. The graze along his head amounted to nothing; it was the shoulder that was serious.

Only it wasn't the shoulder at all, he discovered. The pain had simply settled there. The wound was an inch or two below, actually high in his breast. It had bled freely, front and rear, and from that he knew the bullet had passed entirely through his body. He reckoned he was lucky to that extent.

Again worn out, he slumped forward, supporting himself by his stiffened right arm. The wound was still bleeding and needed attention — but it would have to wait a few more minutes until he could develop enough strength to rig up bandages of some sort.

He thought then of Stokes, of Leggett and Joe Dee Kline. They would be searching for him — at least, they would if they, too, weren't dead or badly shot up. They could be nearby. He raised his head and shouted,

"Stokes! Leggett! Joe Dee!"

There was no reply, not even an echo from the dark, brooding Sacramento canyons. He realized then that his voice was too weak to carry any appreciable distance.

His gun . . . he could fire it a couple of times. . . .

He dropped his hand to his holster. Disappointment and frustration surged through him. The leather was empty. He looked about on the ledge, straining his eyes in the half light. He could see no sign of the pistol. Then he realized he was not on the same ledge at all — that he was below. When shot, he had staggered, then fallen to the next lower shelf of rock. His weapon must be up above.

A brief wave of panic shocked him. The sorrel — where the hell was the sorrel? Without a horse, badly wounded, he was most certainly a dead man, even if he managed to patch himself up. He stared about anxiously, trying to see in the dimness. He could not locate the horse.

Cursing softly, he regained control of himself. *Do things one at a time. . . . Worry about the next problem when you face it. . . . Keep your head. . . .*

He reached up and pulled loose the bandanna he wore about his neck. Holding one corner by his teeth, he ripped it across the center. He paused until his breathing returned to near normal, then folded each half of the cloth into square pads. Then, summoning his strength once more, he slid his right hand under his stiff, encrusted shirt and placed one of the pads upon the wound in his back. Blood accumulated there held it fairly secure.

The second pad he pressed against the opening made by the bullet's entrance. Then, by grasping the folds of his shirt front tightly, he was able to exert pressure and hold the pads firmly in position. They should at least slow down the bleeding until help arrived . . .

Help?

Who could help him? He considered that question soberly. Likely Stokes was dead — along with young Kline and Jim Leggett. And if they were not, they probably were far from where he lay on the ledge by that hour.

He turned his head and looked out onto the mesa, hopefully seeking the small, red eye that would indicate a campfire. If one were visible it would prove that Stokes and the others were in the area. (Or that *someone* was, he thought grimly.) Disappointment again washed over him. There was only the pale, silver glow of the stars and weak moonlight. The light was so inadequate that he could not even tell whether the herd was still there or not. Certainly it should be.

He yelled again, putting all his strength into it, and calling out the names of each of the three men. Once more there was only silence. They were all dead — or they had gone. He was certain his voice could have been heard that time.

He grew drowsy. For a time he fought against the thought of sleep, but finally he gave it up. There was nothing he could do, anyway. He was too weak to walk, and in such a state of exhaustion that if he tried to crawl about on the ledge in the darkness, he could fall again. He doubted if his battered body could stand another physical shock. No . . . stay put . . . get some sleep. In that way he could perhaps rebuild his strength now that the bleeding had been checked. Time enough to think about getting off the ledge when daylight came.

He lay back and was asleep almost immediately. When he opened his eyes again he could feel the sun's blast upon his face and body. Amazed, he realized it was hours past dawn.

Disturbed by that, he sat up, and felt a

glow of satisfaction when the knowledge came to him that he had accomplished that simple act without too much effort and pain. The night's rest had helped considerably.

He turned his attention toward the flat and the grass covered swale where Stokes had intended to bed the herd. It was empty. Surprised, he lifted his glance. Far to the east there appeared to be a thin, yellowish cloud poised above the horizon. It looked like dust, but at such distance he could not be sure.

It was the herd, he concluded. It had to be. Either Stokes had managed to fight off the rustlers and had pushed on with the stock during the night — or the rancher and his two riders were dead and the cattle thieves were in charge.

Regardless, he had to catch up. First, however, he must find the sorrel. Painfully, Wade got to his feet. A surge of dizziness rocked him momentarily, and he stood there, weaving unsteadily until it passed.

He moved then to the edge of the shelf, and glanced about. He could not see below because of a third jutting finger of rock, but there was grass beyond it, he recalled, and if luck were with him, he would find the sorrel there — assuming the big red horse had not been stolen by the rustlers or had trailed along after the herd. He started to make his way along the rocky surface when he recalled his missing gun.

Wade halted, and looked upward. The ledge from which he had tumbled was little more than six feet above. Having little strength and but one usable arm and hand, he worked his way up the short incline to where he had stood. The pistol lay near center. Apparently when the first bullet of the ambusher had grooved across his head, instinct and pure reflex action had sent his hand reaching for the weapon. The impact of the second slug had caused him to drop it.

He recovered the .45, jammed it into its holster and started back down the grade. He fell twice, gritting his teeth with pain each time, but finally he was on the floor of the canyon. Hope leaped high within him when he spotted the sorrel a hundred feet farther on, placidly grazing in a small coulee.

He reached the horse, clawed at the canteen hanging from the saddle and eased his burning thirst. The sorrel whickered anxiously at the smell of the water and he managed, with one hand, to get a few swallows down the beast's throat.

That done, he rested briefly; then, gathering his strength, he pulled himself onto the saddle. The effort cost him consciousness again and for several moments he simply sat there in the blistering sunlight, hand locked about the saddle horn, sucking for breath while his senses floundered in darkness.

Finally that, too, passed. He raised his red rimmed eyes and looked to the east. The dust cloud he had seen — or thought he had seen — was no longer visible. But the herd had to be there somewhere, he was positive of that. And he had to overtake it. Urging the sorrel into motion, he moved out of the wash onto the mesa.

The sack of grub hanging from the horn caught his attention. Immediately he became aware of hunger. And food would help him to recover his strength. He leaned forward stiffly and unhooked the looped cord. His head swam and he caught himself. He was weaker than he had thought — but he'd be fine now. As long as he had his horse and could stick on the saddle, he'd be fine.

But that could be the problem. A warmness on his chest told him the wound had begun to bleed again.

IX

The thick slices of bread and beef tasted good, if somewhat hard and dry. Luke finished one, and eased the thirst it created with another pull at his canteen. He felt some better but he could not shake the leaden weariness that clung to him. He wouldn't, he knew, until he got those bullet holes cared for properly.

The morning, breathlessly hot, dragged into noon. Still he could see no dust, and that mystified as well as alarmed him and turned him impatient. Where the hell was the herd? No man could drive two hundred steers across a flat and through low foothills without raising some dust. Granted, the land was rich sod, covered with grass — but there still should be a little dust.

His mind, wandering slightly and vaguely confused, decided there should have been other things too — a search for him on the part of Helm Stokes when he hadn't shown up at camp, for one thing. The rancher knew where he had gone, knew exactly which point of rock he had intended to climb and make his check of the country. Why hadn't Stokes come for him — or at least sent Joe Dee or Leggett to see what the delay was?

A thread of reason crept into his brain. Maybe Stokes hadn't had the chance; maybe the rustlers had struck too fast and too hard for him to do anything. Maybe Helm Stokes was dead — but he reckoned the rustlers would have had a hard time doing that; they hadn't had much luck getting rid of the big cattleman the last time they'd tried.

He shook his head. Everything was getting fuzzy again. He was sweating freely. He mopped at his face with the back of his right hand, allowing the left to hang stiffly at his side. The damned wound was continuing to ooze. He tried to adjust the pads, but they were stuck tight and he flinched when he sought to change them. He gave it up, swearing vividly in a low, ragged voice.

Still no dust cloud in sight . . . nor had he come upon a hoof beaten trail. The latter he could understand and it did not particularly disturb him; he could be above or below the exact route the cattle had taken across the broad plain. By angling either right or left he could eventually intercept their tracks, but the effort wasn't worth it; he was headed east and he knew that was right.

The lack of dust was something else. There simply had to be a pall, unless — Luke Wade's faltering thoughts came to a full stop — unless the herd was much farther ahead than he had figured. On such solid land with a small bunch of cattle, it was conceivable the dust would not be seen at a long distance.

But he had been no more than a half mile behind the steers when they had been bedded down. True, that next morning he had overslept several hours; the herd could have gotten a good start on him, but hardly sufficient to move completely out of sight.

That left one obvious answer. The herd had been pushed on during the night.

Wade grunted as that conclusion became clear to him. It would have been one hell of a chore, forcing the tired steers on through the darkness. Like most animals, when sundown came, cattle instinctively sought rest. It was their nature, and being contrary, stubborn brutes, they would balk at every attempt to keep them moving. But it could be done if there were enough drovers on hand to keep at them.

He guessed that was what had happened.

The rustlers had taken over the herd, after getting rid of Stokes and Leggett and young Joe Dee Kline. They had figured he, as the guard, was already out of the picture. They had then pushed the stock on for perhaps three or four more hours, getting the herd as far as possible from the immediate vicinity. Knowing the country, they had likely halted in a deep swale where they had rested the cattle until daylight, and then resumed the drive.

That was the way of it, Luke felt sure, and all he need do was keep riding eastward until he caught up. Just what he could do then was unclear in his mind, but he would think of something. . . . The rustlers would be —

Then he saw the body.

Through the shimmering heat waves it was a dark lump on the gray-green of the mesa. A horse waited patiently fifty yards below in the shadow of a twisted cedar tree. Luke eyed the crumpled shape with almost stupid interest for several moments, then roused himself and veered the sorrel to it. His faculties were lagging and somehow he couldn't seem to get himself organized and fully comprehend the meaning of the lifeless shape. But finally it dawned on him that he had found Helm Stokes.

Only it wasn't Stokes. When he had slid painfully from the saddle and crouched beside the dead man, he saw with a sickening shock that it was young Joe Dee Kline.

Luke sat back on his heels, mopped sweat from his face and stared down at Joe Dee's drawn features. The mark of pain lay there — and fear and hope. There were two bullet wounds in his chest. Neither would have killed him instantly. Evidently he had managed to stay on his horse for some time, although unconscious, before he had toppled from the saddle. The pony, naturally, would have continued to follow the herd until its rider fell from its back.

The discovery jolted some measure of reason into Luke Wade's waning senses. He swore deeply while a driving, seething hatred began to build within him, lend him strength and pyramid his determination. Damn a bunch of ruthless bastards who would kill a boy! They could have avoided cutting him down — they could have just wounded him, even scared him off. They hadn't had to murder him.

Stokes and Jim Leggett were something else. He could understand their deaths. They were grown men, capable of handling themselves and able to cope with renegade outlaws on even terms. But a boy like Joe

Dee . . . a youngster . . .

Luke pulled himself to his feet. He would have to do something about the boy's body; he couldn't leave him lying there for the coyotes and buzzards to work over. He steadied himself against the sorrel and glanced around for something with which to dig a grave. There was nothing, not even a length of dry wood. And there were no rocks that could be used to erect a mound.

Sighing deeply as he recognized the task that lay before him, Wade heaved himself onto his saddle, his shoulder screaming at the effort, and moved off toward Joe Dee's mount. He would have to get the boy onto his pony somehow and take him on in to the railhead.

An hour later, almost totally exhausted, sweat pouring off his sagging frame in rivulets, he had the youngster aboard his horse and tied to the saddle. The labor involved cost Luke every ounce of strength he had managed to store up, and he clung weakly to the sorrel, mouth flared, while his lungs gasped for wind.

When he was again able he grasped the cantle of his hull with his right hand and, ignoring the murderous pain in his shoulder, hauled himself onto the red. Nausea claimed him once more but he rode it out, simply sat quietly, head down while his senses reeled.

A drink of water helped. To further aid himself, he removed his sweat stained hat and poured a small quantity of the water onto his head. After that he felt better, and, taking up the reins of Joe Dee's buckskin pony, he pushed on.

Mind clearing, he wondered if it wasn't likely he would encounter Helm Stokes' body, and Leggett's, too, somewhere ahead. If he did there would be nothing he'd be able to do about them but let them lie where they had fallen. He knew he didn't have it in him to hoist even one more body onto a horse.

The heat began to break as the afternoon faded. Ahead he saw the low, dark ridges of another range of mountains, lying directly across his path. They were not tall hills, he noted, and that was some comfort.

Anson's Fork couldn't be too far ahead now. Traveling somewhat faster than a herd of cattle, he would make the trip in considerably less time. That again brought up the question of the lost beef. What had happened to the herd? By all that was normal he should have overtaken it, or at least brought it into sight, by that hour. There was still no sign, no track. And no dust.

But the missing steers had sunk to secondary importance to him now. He thought only of reaching the railhead, turning the body of Joe Dee Kline over to the authorities, and then seeing to his own needs. He was rational enough now to know he could do nothing in his condition.

Maybe the answer would be waiting for him at Anson's Fork. Maybe the cattle would be there and he'd be able to retain consciousness long enough to notify the local lawman. Just how the herd could manage to beat him to the railhead he was not sure, and he had neither the will nor the strength to puzzle it out. But that would come. Later, after he had visited a doctor and got some hot food in his belly, he'd be in shape to put things right. All that counted now was the getting there.

He reached the first outthrusting tongue of the mountains shortly after sunset. He was so near total collapse he was not aware of the deep rose flame that blazed a ribbon across the western horizon, was conscious only that sharp pointed heat lances no longer stabbed into his back and shoulders.

The sorrel began to quicken his pace almost at once, and Luke allowed the horse to have his head. He was too far gone to hold him back anyway.

It was water that drew the sorrel — a wide, ankle deep river that came from the floor of a broad, steep walled canyon and flowed across the trail.

It was a great temptation to drop from the saddle and sprawl full length in the shallow depths of the stream, but Wade resisted the urge, knowing that once off his horse he would be too weak to remount. So he waited.

When the two animals had satisfied their thirst, he goaded the sorrel with his spurs and sent him plodding woodenly on. Things were a little better now. The heat was gone and a faint breeze had sprung up, slipping quietly in from the southeast, fanning his face and relieving some of the fire that seemed to be running wild in his body.

Hours later — he had no real conception of time — his feverish eyes caught sight of lights far in the distance. His pulse quickened and he struggled to sit straighter on the saddle. But he was too weak for even that, and he compromised by simply riding hunched forward, peering anxiously into the darkness from beneath the tipped brim of his hat.

The sorrel seemed to move with incredible, aggravating slowness, and for a time the small yellow dots hanging in the night stood still, and he could draw no nearer. Each rise the lagging sorrel mastered seemed to be only one of a thousand more than lay between him and his destination.

Frequently he dozed, always unwillingly, exhausted in body and mind, and then finally he roused to discover that the sorrel had gained a crest of a hill and stopped. Below, at the foot of the slope, were the first of the lights.

A harsh croak burst from Luke Wade's burning throat. He dug his spurs deep into the horse's flanks, cursing the animal unreasonably. At once the sorrel started down the gentle grade, moving at a tired trot.

They reached level ground and Luke aimed the horse at the nearest of the houses where a lamp shone softly through a window. He reached the gate, turned into the yard and halted in the square of light flung out into the darkness.

Mustering the shreds of his strength, he called out, "Hello, the house. . . ."

He remembered the door swinging open, was aware of the sudden splash of more light — and that was all.

X

Oddly, it was the familiar odor of a strong antiseptic that brought Luke to consciousness.

There had been a bottle of it at home. Introduced by surgeons near the close of the war, it had proved most effective. Upon discharge Ben Wade had obtained a small quantity of the potent germ killer and taken it with him. He had kept it on the shelf with other medicines and remedies and Luke had used it often for cuts and abrasions sustained while working around the ranch.

Wade looked around. He lay on a narrow bed, covered by a clean, white sheet. It was a small room, skimpily furnished. A window in the wall opposite was open and a curtain waved gently in the fitful breeze. It was shortly after sundown, Luke guessed.

He stirred, trying to sit up. Pain raced through his body and his left shoulder and arm were rigid. He glanced down. A neatly applied bandage encircled his chest and extended onto his arm. He frowned, and lay back. Lifting his right hand, he touched his head. It, too, was bandaged.

At that moment the door opened. A man in a knee-length white coat paused there and looked down on him. He had a round face, dark hair combed tight to his skull. A thin moustache covered his upper lip, an obvious attempt to create the illusion of greater age. He could be only a few years older than he, Wade guessed.

"I'm Doctor David," the man in the coat said. "Hope you're feeling better."

Luke said, "I am. Reckon I can thank you for that." He hesitated, frowning. "Can't seem to remember getting here."

David stepped forward briskly and made a few quick adjustments of the bandages. "One of the neighbors brought you. Said you rode into his yard, yelled, and fell off your horse. He and his boy carried you here to my office. You were in mighty bad shape."

"It was a long ride," Luke murmured. Then: "Did somebody take care of the boy's body?"

"All looked after. Lucky you aren't lying in a pine box at the coroner's, too. Hungry?"

Wade shook his head, surprised at himself. "No, not much. Could use some coffee."

"Expect you'd better eat anyway. You lost a lot of blood, and steak and potatoes are the best way I know of to get it back." David drew back, turning toward the door. Halfway into the adjoining room he halted and looked over his shoulder. "Almost forgot. Marshal wants to talk to you. Said for me to call him when you regained consciousness. Feel up to it?"

Luke said, "Sure, why not? Expect he wants to know what happened — and I got plenty to tell him."

The physician disappeared into the shadows. Luke heard him say something to someone unseen, and then the outer door opened and closed. He turned his head to the side and stared through the window. Lamps were being lit along Anson's Fork's main street, and the night's activities were stirring into life. There was the faint smell of dust in the still warm air, and somewhere a jackass brayed in raucous discord.

A heaviness came over him. He had failed the Mangus Valley ranchers, he realized bitterly. Instead of getting their herd through, he had lost it — along with the lives of Joe Dee, Stokes and Jim Leggett. A hell of a mess he had made of it. Right now those two hundred steers should have been in Anson's Fork's cattle pens, and he and the others should have been celebrating and preparing for the return trip. Instead —

The door opened again, and closed softly. The sound of boot heels crossing a barren floor followed, and then abruptly an elderly man wearing a star stood in the doorway. Doctor David was at his shoulder.

"Our town marshal, Amos Spilman," the physician said. "Never did find out your name."

"Wade . . . Luke Wade."

"Luke Wade, Amos. You've got about ten minutes. He's not up to much talking yet."

"Won't take me long," Spilman said in a quick, business-like way. He entered the room and stood at the end of the cot, a tall, wide shouldered man with deep creases in his weathered face.

"Where you hail from, Wade?"

"Red Hill — the Mangus Valley country. I was bringing —"

"Who was the dead man you brought in, and who shot him?"

"Name is Joe Dee Kline. Son of one of the ranchers. Rustlers got him — along with two other men making the drive. Came close to finishing me."

"Rustlers?" Spilman echoed, pulling his face into a frown. "Where'd they jump you?"

"This side of the Sacramentos."

"How many in the party?"

Wade shrugged, and winced at the pain the movement caused. "Don't know. Never did see them. I got bushwhacked right off the start."

Spilman's features were flat, expressionless. He strolled to the window, brushed the curtain aside and stared into the street. Without turning, he said, "Those other two men — who were they? How come you didn't bring them in, too?"

"Didn't run across their bodies — and if I had I'd never have got them loaded on their horses. Was all I could do to bring in Joe Dee. Names were Stokes and Leggett."

The lawman turned. "Then you ain't sure they're dead . . . for certain, I mean."

"Pretty sure," Luke replied, anger beginning to lift within him. "They killed Joe Dee, tried their best to kill me, and ran off with our herd. They had to do something with Stokes and Leggett, didn't they?"

The marshal nodded absently. "Seems so," he said.

"Then I figure you're wasting time. How about getting up a posse and heading west toward the Sacramentos. Bound to come across the herd out there somewhere — if they haven't already been driven here."

"Been no stock brought in for a week,"

the lawman said.

"Then they're still out there. You find the herd and you'll find the killers, too. And if you do a little looking you ought to come across Stokes and Leggett. They'll be some-where between —"

Luke's words trailed off. Spilman was wagging his head in a slow, positive way.

"What's the matter?"

"Not much I can do about it," the law-man said. "I'm just the town marshal. Got no authority outside Anson's Fork."

"Then who the hell can I talk to?"

"Sheriff, I reckon."

"He here in town?"

"Nope. Office is in Lincoln."

"Lincoln!" Luke repeated wearily. "That's more'n a hundred miles away."

"Afraid so. I'm real sorry, son, but it sure don't look like there's much I can do for you and that herd you say you lost."

"I lost it — along with three friends," Wade snapped. He sank back, suddenly exhausted. "Devil of a note," he muttered. "You've got law here — only you haven't."

Amos Spilman lifted his arms and allowed them to drop in a gesture of resignation. "Like I said, I've got no authority 'cepting here in town. Now, you get them rustlers and bring them in to me, and I'll sure as hell jail them for you."

"Be a little hard to do, me laying here in bed," Wade said sarcastically. He shifted his glance to David. "How long before I can get out of here, Doc?"

The physician pursed his lips. "Expect you've already tried to sit up — and you got your answer right then. You're plenty weak. Ought to stay where you are a couple more days at least. Three wouldn't hurt. Even then you'll have to take it slow."

"Wish there was something I could do," Spilman said lamely. "I —"

"It's real important I get moving," Luke said, ignoring the lawman. "Fix me up, Doc. I can't hang around here no later than morning."

David cocked his head to one side. "I'll sure do what I can, but I won't guarantee much. However, you're a pretty healthy specimen in spite of what you've been through. Let's get some more good food in your belly and see how you feel tomorrow."

"By then I'll be fine," Luke said.

Spilman edged toward the door. "What do you want me to do about the dead man?"

"Hold the body. His folks'll probably want to bury him on their ranch."

Spilman groaned. "Ain't hardly got no place —"

"Use Hardyman's ice house," David broke in. "They just hauled in some ice from the cave."

"Reckon I could do that," the marshal said, moving on. He halted in the doorway. "Sure sorry there ain't nothing I can do for you, Wade."

"You might just take yourself a ride out west, sort of passing the time," Luke suggested. "Could be you'd come across the bodies of my friends. Don't think that'd be jumping your authority, would it?"

Spilman gave him a quiet look, shrugged and left the room. David crossed to the window and peered out.

"It's taking them long enough to bring that meal," he grumbled. "Going to get myself a woman one of these days just so I can get my cooking down here at home. Think I'll trot over and see if I can hurry it up."

The doctor wheeled and disappeared into the other part of the house. Wade lay motionless, mulling over his conversation with Spilman. He would get no help there; that was clear to him now. What was to be done would have to be done on his own — and soon.

One thing was sure: the herd was still back on the flats somewhere. It couldn't just have been swallowed up. And Helm Stokes and Leggett; he'd have to find their bodies, too. It wasn't decent to let them lie out there in the sun, bloating, to become food for the carrion-eaters.

He pulled himself to a sitting position despite the waves of pain that slugged him. David said he might be in shape to get up that next morning. Luke clamped his jaw shut; it was up to him to make it possible.

Resting his back against the wood panels of the bed's headboard, he tried to move his left arm. The muscles were stiff, seemed frozen into place. Pain racked him at each attempt to move it but he weathered each onslaught and kept doggedly at it. After a few moments he was able to raise the arm slightly.

Encouraged, he began to flex the muscles, twist and work his wrist. Then the elbow. Gradually his arm began to loosen, but now his shoulder was flaming with pain.

He heard David enter the house, and paused. The physician came into the room bearing a tray upon which was a plate heaped with steak, potatoes, fried eggs, hot biscuits and butter. A small granite coffee pot, steaming and full, and with a cup, were alongside. There was also a water tumbler half filled with raw whiskey. David gave

Luke a swift scrutiny.

"I see you're already at it," he said, and placed the tray on Wade's lap. "That's fine . . . just don't overdo it."

He picked up the knife and fork and cut the meat into small squares. That done, he stepped back.

"Get that down first," he said, pointing at the liquor. "Then eat. I've been pouring gruel down you ever since you got here, but you need something solid that'll stick to your ribs. I'll look in on you later — and when I do I want to see that plate licked clean. Understand?"

Luke grinned. "Sure — I understand."

David bobbed his head, and again pursed his lips. "Maybe, just maybe, we'll have you on your feet by daylight."

XI

It must have been the whiskey that put the starch back into his muscles, Luke Wade decided that next morning when he arose, somewhat shakily, and began to pull on his clothing. The good food and the expert ministrations of Doc David could not be discounted, of course, but there was no denying the fire the raw liquor had built within his body.

It was an effort to dress but he kept at it doggedly until, gun at his hip, he was ready to go about the plans he had earlier formulated. He started for the door, reeled dangerously, and caught himself by bracing his right hand against the wall. He grinned wolfishly. He wasn't as strong as he'd thought.

Resting briefly, he made his way into the adjoining room, and found it empty. He heard noises out in the back yard and fumbled his way to the open doorway. David was watering a small garden planted against a weathered fence. The physician glanced up as Luke halted in the opening. He smiled.

"You've got more guts than an army mule. A wound like that would keep an ordinary man in bed for a week."

"Not if he had things to 'tend to," Wade replied. "Like to settle up with you, be on my way."

David put the watering can aside and moved toward Luke. "First I'll have a look at things," he said. "Didn't expect you up quite so early. . . . Sit over there."

"Already lost too damn much time," Wade grumbled, backing into the room and sinking onto a hardbacked chair.

"You rush things too fast and you'll find yourself in that bed again," the physician warned.

"I aim to take it easy."

David made no answer. Using a pair of scissors, he snipped the bandage encircling Luke's head. With gentle fingers he examined the angry groove left by the bullet.

"That'll do fine," he said. "Just don't scratch it. Now, pull off your shirt so I can see the other little souvenirs your friends gave you."

Wade complied. David removed the bandage. Lips pursed in his habitual manner, the doctor probed the two lesions thoughtfully.

"Good, good," he murmured. "They'll be all right if you don't pull some fool stunt and break them open."

He left the room momentarily, and returned with a tray of bottles and fresh bandages. Quickly and efficiently, he dressed the wound, applying more antiseptic and a cooling salve.

"I'll leave the bandage a bit looser this time," he said. "Closure is not important now. Just a matter of healing." Finished, he stepped back. "What do you plan on doing?"

"Soon as I run down that cattle buyer we were supposed to meet here, I'm heading west. Got to locate the herd if I can. Lot of people depending on the money from the sale."

David shook his head. "Riding's not going to do you any good. Apt to break that wound open again."

"Can't be helped," Luke said, reaching into his pocket. "How much I owe you?"

"How about two-fifty? Suit you?"

Wade produced his supply of change and counted out the specified amount. "Fine with me, but it hardly seems enough. Fact is, I'd double it if I had the cash, but you're looking at my pile."

"Two-fifty's the going rate, and I don't believe in sticking the cash customers just because everybody else is on credit." He thrust the money into his pocket. "Wait here; I'll bring up your horse."

Luke followed the physician out into the yard. "I owe you for his keep, too, don't I?"

David grinned. "It's on the house. Everybody, mostly pays me in hay and grain. If I had ten horses they couldn't live long enough to eat up what I've got stored in my barn. What about the boy's buckskin?"

"Be obliged if you'll let him stay. I'll have somebody pick him up."

David nodded and disappeared into a small, sagging structure at the rear of his lot. Within a few minutes he returned leading the sorrel. He passed the reins to Luke.

"Be smart now. Go easy."

Wade grinned, and pulled himself carefully onto the saddle. His left arm and shoulder were still somewhat stiff, but on the whole he didn't feel too bad. There was just the weakness.

David said, "The cattle buyer you're looking for will be at the hotel — there's only one in town. Likely find him at the restaurant right next door, this time of the morning."

Wade nodded, and headed on to the dusty street. He paused there, vaguely dizzy, and scanned the double line of high and low false-fronted buildings that strung off to his left. *The Westerner Hotel* was about half way down. A cafe sign hung above the plank walk just beyond. He swung the sorrel toward it.

Pulling in to the hitchrack he dismounted awkwardly, wrapped the leathers around the crossbar, and entered the restaurant. It was a small place, no more than half a dozen tables and a short counter. A waitress in a starched apron looked up at him expectantly.

"I'm hunting that cattle buyer," Wade said, coming straight to the point. "He been here yet?"

The woman smiled. "No — but he's about due."

"I'll wait for him at that back table," Luke said, motioning at a back corner. "And while I'm waiting, bring me something to eat. Double order of eggs and bacon. And a pot of coffee."

"Yes, sir," the waitress said, then frowned as Wade staggered slightly. "You all right, mister?"

"All right," he muttered, and moved for the corner table.

Wade had just begun to eat when a nattily dressed individual, wearing a derby hat cocked to one side, entered. Smiling brightly, the waitress hurried to him. She spoke a few words, pointing to Luke. Apparently this was the man he wanted to see.

The buyer made his way through the tables, halted before Wade and extended his hand. "Name's Bishop. Hear you're looking for me."

"If you buy cattle, I am," Wade said, shaking hands. He introduced himself and Bishop sat down. Luke explained what had happened to the Mangus Valley herd.

Bishop toyed with his gold watch chain. "Too bad. I was expecting it in today. Guess there's no point in hanging around any longer."

"That's what I wanted to talk to you about," Luke said, leaning forward. "I'm asking you to give me a few more days. That herd's out there somewhere, and I'm heading out to find it and bring it in."

"Maybe," the buyer said doubtfully. "Rustlers have a way of disappearing quick with the steers they've grabbed."

"Maybe so — but hell — two hundred steers don't just fade into nothing!"

"You any idea where they might be?"

"A little. I remember crossing a shallow river west of here —"

"That'll be the Penasco. About twenty, twenty-five miles out."

"Laying in that bed at Doc David's I had a chance to do some thinking. I've got a hunch I'll find a trail somewhere along that river."

Bishop wagged his head. "That'll take you three or four days, maybe a week. And for two hundred head it's hardly worth my while to wait."

"It's mighty important to those people back in the valley that this sale goes through," Luke said earnestly. "And it could mean plenty to you later on. It's a small herd, sure, and you're dealing with small ranchers. But little ranches grow into big ones — and you'd be putting yourself in strong with every one of them. They wouldn't forget the favor and I expect you'd have first crack at every head they raised in the future."

Bishop stroked his moustache, and cast a sidelong glance at the smiling waitress. "Well . . . if you're putting it that way, I might just hang around until Saturday. . . ."

"I'll appreciate it," Wade said, relaxing slightly. "You won't regret it."

"Always happy to help new ranchers get on their feet," Bishop said expansively. "Pays off eventually. Now, if you'll excuse me, I'll have my breakfast."

Luke opened his mouth, intending to invite the cattle buyer to sit with him, but Bishop was looking at the waitress, who stood expectantly beside a table on the opposite side of the room.

"All set, then," he said as the man rose. "I'll see you by Saturday, if not before."

Bishop bobbed his head. "Good luck. I don't know how you can manage it, but I'll wait around to see if you do."

"I'll manage it," Luke replied quietly. "I've got to."

XII

The heat was brutal. Piercing rays, like sharp, white-hot lances, speared from a cloudless sky, stabbed into him, and steadily drained the juices from his already weakened body.

His shoulder pained considerably and he learned that when it became unbearable, relief was to be had by dismounting and walking ahead of the sorrel for a time. It slowed his progress, but conversely, it served also to rebuild his lagging strength.

As a result it was noon when he reached the Penasco River. Luke had intentionally swung to the south, determined to search along the banks of the stream for prints of the stolen cattle. He didn't believe the rustlers had cut to that direction — it was logical to assume they had veered northward — but he was bucking a time deadline and he could not afford to whip back and forth endlessly searching for the trail.

He halted at the broad, shallow stream and spent a quarter hour soaking his head, washing his face and neck in the cool water while the sorrel took his fill. He felt much better after the refreshing pause, and soon moved on.

Crossing to the Penasco's west bank, he headed upstream, his eyes now on the soft mud under the sorrel's hoofs. Although events subsequent to the ambush were hazy in his mind, he was fairly certain the herd had been driven across the river, and not turned north along the west slopes of the low lying hills.

Unless they had been driven up the Penasco.

His thoughts came to an abrupt halt at that possibility. . . . Up the river, between the walls of the canyon through which it flowed. The stream was shallow, scarcely hoof deep, and soft earth, covered with grass and the flat-leafed cone-centered plant they called *cow-slips* back home, extended back on either side for several yards. It would have been simple to drive a herd up the canyon.

Eager now, he urged the sorrel to a slow lope, ignoring the pain in his shoulder. Somewhere ahead he would intersect the hundreds of hoof prints left by the cattle; if

111

he were right, they would march up to the edge of the river and there disappear.

Minutes later his probing eyes picked up the tracks left by his sorrel and Joe Dee Kline's horse where they had crossed two nights previous. The imprints had crusted over — but they were there. Encouraged, he hurried on.

The flat began to lift and meet the slopes of the low string of hills, bringing to Luke Wade a faint doubt. He was drawing nearer to the first bluffs marking the mouth of the canyon. Unless he encountered the trail left by the herd soon, he would have to conclude that he was wrong, and that the rustlers had followed some other course.

But the tracks were there — hundreds of deep-cut imprints in a narrow band. The herd had entered the river and the canyon at the very foot of the opening.

Relief flowing through him, Luke Wade halted and swung from the saddle. He ground reined the sorrel at the base of the bluffs and walked slowly upstream, eyes scanning the spongy green earth. For the first hundred feet he saw nothing, but now there was no doubt in his mind and so he pressed on.

A short distance later, hoof prints began to appear on the Penasco's banks. It was clear then what had happened: the cattle had waded the stream for a time, then begun to string out on solid ground. Here and there he spotted droppings, and with that final assurance, Luke turned about and retraced his steps to the sorrel. He had only to follow the river through the canyon, and eventually he would come to the missing herd.

It was pleasant within the confines of the walls. Squat cedars, pinons and scrub oak brush dotted the rocky slopes and now and then bright splashes of vivid reds, yellows and whites marked beds of wildflowers.

The floor of the canyon, fifty feet wide on the average and nearly level, was covered with grass and other lush growth that softened the heat and made the passage easy for both Wade and the sorrel.

Gray squirrels darted in and out of the rocks, and white breasted bluebirds and sharp tongued jays with their arrogant crests uplifted flitted ahead of him. Several times the sorrel's progress disturbed drab gray dipperbirds, teetering on stones in midstream, and sent them skimming off, barely clearing the water.

The canyon twisted continually, never becoming deeper or more shallow. The sun dropped below the rim to the west and long shadows began to stretch across the stream. It was still hours until sunset, Luke knew, but darkness would come early along the bottom of the canyon.

He grew hungry and ate again from the sack of grub old Caleb had prepared. Coffee would have helped considerably, but he was reluctant to stop and build a fire. Smoke might reveal his presence. He had no idea, of course, how far ahead the herd might be. He had lost a day and two nights at Anson's Fork in addition to the time spent riding back and forth. Unless the rustlers had halted somewhere along the way, he could have a long ride before him.

It ended much sooner than he had hoped.

The canyon angled sharply to the left a half mile farther on. He made the turn, the sorrel trotting slowly along at the edge of the water, and pulled up short when he beheld a wide, sunlit mesa stretching out beyond the end of the hills.

Immediately he swung the horse away from the river, gained higher ground and spurred him into a lope, anxious to see what lay beyond the canyon's northern mouth. When he reached the wide opening, he again halted. A low whistle escaped his lips.

A deep swale, at least a mile across, lay to his left, a lush, circular oasis on the surface of the prairie. Tall, thick trunked cotton-wood trees spread their branches over the entire area and at the lower end an ample watering pond shimmered in the afternoon light.

Near the center stood a squat ranch house. Four horses waited, hip shot and heads low, at the hitchrack fronting it. Farther back Luke could see a barn and a scatter of outbuildings. And in the corral, shifting restlessly, were the missing cattle.

XIII

Luke Wade assumed it was the stolen herd. There appeared to be about two hundred head, and the trail out of the canyon led toward the ranch. But it was too far to be positive — and closer inspection would be impossible until darkness fell.

He rode the sorrel off to one side and drew up behind a tangled clump of junipers. There he would be visible neither from the house nor to a rider who might chance to come out of the canyon. He swung stiffly from the saddle, suddenly excessively tired and wishing for a drink of whiskey, or at least some strong coffee to bolster his sagging strength, but both were out of the question.

He ate again, sparingly, from his supply of food, washing down the hard bread and now paper-dry beef with water from his canteen. The sorrel contented himself with browsing on the thin grass growing in the open spaces between the rocks.

Just what he would or could do was not clear in Luke Wade's mind. He had tracked down the stolen cattle, the proof of which he would obtain as soon as night came, but from there on his course was uncertain.

One thing was clear: he had to get the beef to Anson's Fork as soon as possible. Bishop would not wait much longer — certainly not beyond the Saturday deadline he had stated. And while the herd below was, at that point, likely little more than a long day's drive from the settlement, there was not time enough to return to Red Hill, gather the ranchers concerned and bring them in to help. The same held true with the railhead.

And he could not do it alone. No one man, however expert and experienced, could manage two hundred obstinate steers by himself. He shook his head, disturbed by the problem — and then dismissed it from his mind. He would find some way to meet the issue when the moment came.

Finished with his sparse meal, he hung the sack back on the saddle and, favoring his wounded shoulder, climbed to a somewhat higher ledge on the side of the hill where he could look out over the mesa and see the ranch.

The sun was falling slowly into a blaze of golds and yellows beyond the Sacramentos, and long streaks of clouds hovering about the peaks and ridges were assuming varying shades of purple. As he watched the fiery glow spread, until it extended the full, sprawling length of the great hills, which grew steadily darker beneath the changing purples.

Back in the canyon a dove cooed mournfully and a squirrel chattered. Up on the slope something moved — a rabbit, most likely — and a small cascade of gravel spilled over a ledge, disturbing the hush. A door slammed, the slap of it hollow and distant.

Instantly Wade turned his attention to the ranchhouse. A man, carrying a water bucket, came off the rear porch, slammed a second, screened door and entered the yard. He walked lazily to the well a dozen paces to the back of the structure. Placing the bucket on the sill, he began to crank the windlass, setting up a dry squeal that echoed through the quiet. The sorrel paused in his foraging, looked up inquiringly, and then resumed his chore.

The outlaw slopped his bucket full from the keg he had lifted from the depths of the well, turned and started for the house. He gained the porch. The screen slammed once more — but there was no second slap. He had left the inside door, probably leading into the kitchen, open. In deference to the heat, Luke supposed.

Smoke began to trickle from the chimney at that end of the house. It was meal time and the men were preparing to eat. Minutes later yellow lamplight blossomed in a corner window of the same room.

Luke glanced toward the Sacramentos. The sun was entirely gone and the golden glow had turned to a leaden gray — but it was still too light to move in closer.

An hour later, with his shoulder paining in a persistent, aching manner, he watched the lamp go out in the kitchen and come alive again in an adjoining room. The outlaws had completed their meal and had moved into other quarters where they would pass the evening playing cards, drinking and swapping stories. It should be safe enough now to move out, he judged. He was anxious to have a look at the cattle.

Returning to the sorrel, he crawled onto the saddle and cut back. Circling wide across the mesa, he waited until the bulky shape of the barn stood between him and the ranchhouse, and then rode directly forward.

He reached the weathered structure, halted and again dismounted. A tautness gripped him as he secured the sorrel to a tough, squat cedar. He paused, an odd thought crossing his mind: *I've gone through six kinds of hell — and now I'm risking my neck for a man I'm going to kill. Makes no sense. . . .*

He stood there in the dim light, half crouched, considering that truth, wondering at his own inconsistency. And then he eased his outraged sensibilities by telling himself there were other men involved, good men, honest men who deserved his help. It was wrong to penalize the whole of Mangus Valley because of one evil member.

He moved on then, working his way along the splintery boards toward the corrals. He could hear no sounds issuing from the house and concluded the outlaws were unusually quiet or else had turned in for the night. Perhaps they were all in a drunken stupor. He grinned wryly at that bit of wishful thinking; a man just didn't run in that kind of good luck.

He gained the corral, where the cattle heaved and shoved restlessly. Drawing in close, he hurriedly examined the nearest flank for its brand. It was a bold A-D, freshly burned. There was no doubt in his mind now. The steer belonged to Albert Dunn. It was the stolen herd.

He pulled back into the deep shadow of a cottonwood and studied the house. Light still showed in the dusty square of the window and there was yet fire in the kitchen range, judging from the trail of smoke winding lazily into the night sky. It was probably a hangover from coals still alive in the stove, Luke guessed. Such men would spend little time cooking; they would boil coffee and fry meat, but other than that they would have no use for a stove.

Still undecided as to his next move, he slipped in closer to the house, dodging from shadow to shadow, always careful to avoid the open areas. There was no way of telling if any of the men were looking out, and he took no chances. Reaching the structure, he eased up close to the lighted window and peered in.

There were four men, as he had concluded earlier from the number of horses at the rack. They were grouped about a table, engaged in a desultory game of poker. Small piles of matches served as chips.

Surprise rippled through Luke when he recognized one as the redheaded friend of Del's. Red was the man who had hurriedly departed when invited to take up the fight where Del and the Mexican had left off. The others were strangers to Wade; all were hard faced, whiskered men with the stamp of outlaw upon them.

"Reckon we better be gettin' at them steers, come mornin'," one of the men said, laying down his dog-eared cards and reaching for a sack of cigarette makings. "Be a helluva job, workin' over them brands."

"What's the rush?" the rider sitting at his left demanded. "We got plenty of time. Besides, Jim'll be here tomorrow or next day. He can help. Five of us'll do it quicker'n four."

"Suits me," the man with the tobacco said. "I ain't honin' to get at it any more'n you. I recollect up —"

"All right, Todd, you playin' or ain't you?" Red cut in impatiently. "Either bet or back off."

"I'm playin'," Todd said calmly. "Openin' for two bucks." He tossed the necessary matches into the center of the table, then settled his small, dark eyes on the redhead. "You're mighty jumpy. Somethin' eatin' you?"

Red glared at his cards, swore in disgust and slammed them onto the table. "All that's eatin' me is my stinkin' luck . . . and this waitin' around."

"That and thinkin' about how his pal Del got his guts blowed out by that drifter. That sort o' thing sure can get to a man. . . ."

"Well, you're square with him now," the fourth rider said. "He's cold turkey, layin' back there in the hills. By now the buzzards'll have picked him clean."

Red picked up his cards, grunted, and settled back. He seemed relieved. "Expect you're right, Chino. He's been paid off and I got to quit thinkin' about it." He shifted his attention to the fourth man. "Willie, there any more rotgut in that there bottle?"

Willie reached down and held aloft an empty quart bottle. "Nary a drop," he said. "Been sucked bone dry."

Red swore softly. "Nothin' to do but wait — and nothin' to drink while we're doin' that. Damn if I ain't ridin' in to the Forks tomorrow and gettin' a jug."

"Jim'll be bringin' some," Todd assured him. "You'd be makin' the trip for nothin'." He leaned back, yawned. "Gettin' powerful sleepy. How about you birds — want to quit?"

"Couple more hands and I'm ready," Chino said. "Whose bet?"

Luke Wade stepped back from the window. A plan was taking shape in his mind — a wild, desperate plan in which the odds would be stacked high against him; but it was one that could work if he were careful.

He faded into the shadows and made his way to the barn. On impulse, he entered the wide, open doorway, halting just inside. A pile of hay at the far end of the runway, offering itself as a comfortable bed for the night. He could use some rest.

He crossed over and examined the window behind it. The sash was loose in the frame, held in place only by two rusting nails. Pushing them aside, he lifted the window out and leaned it against the wall. It was an instinctive precaution: he now had an escape exit other than the door if anything went wrong.

The sorrel was almost directly below the window; taking up a quantity of hay, he dropped it where the big red could reach it. That done, he made himself comfortable in the corner, prepared to rest and work out the details of the plan he had in mind.

Immediately his pulse quickened as his ears picked up the slow beat of approaching horses. He had overlooked the fact that the four animals out front would likely be stabled for the night.

He thought of the window, but decided it was too late for that — his injured shoulder would hinder him too much if he endeavored to make a hasty escape. He lay back, drew his gun and pulled hay across his prone body, leaving only his eyes exposed. Nerves taut, he watched the doorway.

It was Chino. Lantern in hand, leading the horses, he stepped into the runway. He paused briefly to hang the light on a peg, then continued on. No danger, Wade thought, then felt fresh alarm when he saw that the outlaw was not putting the horses in stalls but was bringing them on to the pile of hay.

Scarcely breathing, Luke watched as Chino came in close — no more than half a dozen paces away — and stopped. He dropped the reins to the floor and moved in behind the animals. Shouldering his way between them, the outlaw slapped them sharply on the rump, forcing them in to where they could help themselves to the hay. He did not trouble to remove the bridles or loosen the girths.

Chino paused beside one of the horses, evidently his own, and began to fiddle with the saddle, making some repair or adjustment. The moments dragged. As he lay tense and rigid, Luke's shoulder began to throb more acutely. He needed to shift his position slightly to relieve the pain but he dared not move. To do so would startle the horses and reveal his presence to Chino.

The rustler worked with aggravating slowness. The weak light of the lantern was behind him and Wade could see his jaws moving methodically as he chewed on a cud of tobacco. One of the horses lifted his head. Luke froze, not even breathing. The animal had picked up his scent, and now stared suspiciously at the mound of hay that Wade had drawn over his body.

At that moment Chino completed his chore and stepped back. The horse lowered his long head, gathered in another mouthful of dry fodder and began to grind it between his teeth. Luke felt the tension ease. The outlaw turned and retraced his steps down the runway, his boot heels rapping a lazy cadence on the hard packed soil. He retrieved the lantern and stepped out into the yard. There was a loud squeak as he closed the doors, a faint jingle of metal when he fastened the hasp.

Luke changed his position, easing the pain. All four horses jumped at the unexpected movement, but he gave it no thought. He could still hear Chino walking toward the house.

He pulled himself about until he lay facing the window. He needed to keep close tab on the hours. When the first hint of light broke in the east, it would be time to start. His plan could prove a death trap if he waited too long.

XIV

Luke Wade got little sleep. The vital importance of timing to his scheme, and the dull, infuriating pain in his shoulder, combined to keep him restless and wakeful. He dozed for only short periods, awaking each time with a start to stare anxiously at the window.

Finally, in disgust, he gave it up and, rising, brushed the hay from his clothing and moved to the opening in the wall. The outlaws' horses, frightened, shied away at his abrupt appearance, but after a few moments they quieted. Since Chino had closed and locked the doors he was forced now to use the window. Slowly and painfully he hoisted himself through the empty framework and dropped to the ground.

It was an hour or more yet until first light, but he was going ahead with his plan, regardless; better to be early than late.

Releasing the sorrel, he led him around the barn to the corral where the cattle were gathered. He tethered the horse to a small tree a few paces back from the enclosure, and then returned to the barn. Using utmost care, he opened one of the doors, doing it slowly to minimize the squeak of hinges. The rusting metal set up a dry screech, nevertheless, but the sound was suppressed and he doubted if anyone had heard it.

There were rifles slung from the saddles of two of the rustlers' horses. Pulling both free, he levered one and assured himself that it was fully loaded. The other he tossed into the pile of hay. He examined the saddlebags next, but found no hidden weapons in any of them. Gathering up the trailing reins of the four animals, he led them to the corral.

Side by side, he tied them to the top bar of the pole enclosure, placing them at a point where they stood near but in front of his own sorrel. He hung the rifle upon his saddle, then turned to study the house.

It lay in complete darkness. Smoke no longer drifted from the kitchen chimney and he guessed the fire was finally out. He waited out a long minute; then, taking a deep breath and pulling his pistol, he moved toward the rear door, hopeful that it had not been closed and barred by the outlaws.

He reached the screen and stepped cautiously onto the porch. A sigh slipped from his tight lips. The door to the kitchen stood open. Holding to the screen to prevent its slamming, he allowed it to swing shut, then crossed the dust covered board floor and entered the house.

Trapped heat still hung heavily in the small room, along with the odor of well boiled coffee. Luke, eyes straining into the darkness, glanced hungrily at the stove, wishing he dared pause for a cup, but he decided against it: the most dangerous part of his plan was before him, and until he had that mastered all else would have to wait.

Holstering his gun, he leaned down and removed his boots. Again taking out the weapon, he crossed the kitchen, weakly lit by moon and starlight, and passed through the opening that led into the room where he had earlier watched the outlaws at their card game.

It was deserted. He had half expected to find some of the men asleep in chairs or on the sagging couch placed against the wall; snoring sounds deeper in the house, however, bespoke bedrooms. On silent feet he made his way along a narrow hall toward the noise.

The outlaws had quartered themselves in two rooms. Halting in the doorway of the first, he recognized Red and the one called

130

Todd. They were sprawled on a ragged bed, sleeping soundly despite the stuffy, sweat-permeated air. Chino and Willie would be farther down the corridor. Luke grinned tightly into the darkness. It made things easier.

Quietly, careful not to stumble against a chair or some other item of furniture, Wade crept into the room. Halting in the center, he looked about, peering through the faint light. Red and his companion lay motionless, only partly unclad. A moment later he saw what he was searching for — the outlaws' gun belts. They hung from the bedpost.

He stepped in silently, lifted them without sound, and backed to the doorway. Both belts were heavy with cartridges, and supporting them with his left hand brought quick pain to his shoulder. He returned to the kitchen and looked for a place in which to hide the weapons. His glance picked up the flour barrel. Lifting the lid, he dumped the equipment into the half full container.

He went then to the room where Chino and Willie slept, followed a similar procedure and dropped back to the kitchen. Removing one of the revolvers, he thrust it into his own belt, thus providing himself with an extra weapon, and then added the remainder to the barrel.

Breathless from tension and effort, he sank onto one of the hard backed chairs. That much was over with. Now, if he could pull off the rest . . .

He drew on his boots and lit the lamp. Taking up the chair and light, he moved to the corner of the room nearest the inside door. There he placed the lamp on a shelf behind and somewhat above. He considered that for a few moments, and decided he was in the best possible position for the outlaws when they came into the room, since he would be to their backs, more or less. This would afford him a favorable advantage. Satisfied, he sat down to wait out another hour.

The smell of coffee beckoned to him. Rising, Luke moved to the stove and laid his hand against the side of the smoke streaked pot. It was lukewarm. Picking up a cup, he poured it full and lifted it to his lips.

It was strong and the bitterness of it jolted him like a blow to the belly, but it scattered the cobwebs gathering about his brain and brought him to a full alert. He glanced out the window. It was still too dark to begin; he had to have enough light to see by.

Taking the pot and cup with him, he returned to his chair and sat down. Refilling the tin container with the last of the pot's contents, he nursed it until the darkness beyond the doorway began to fade. He got to his feet then, and turned down the lamp. Drawing back into the corner as far as the walls would permit, he lifted the metal coffee pot and hurled it through the window.

At the sudden crash, yells erupted in the bedrooms. A gun in each hand, Luke Wade stood poised, waiting, listening to the utter confusion the shattering glass had evoked. Todd was cursing in a wild, steady way. He could hear Chino shouting questions, Red answering. Moments later there was the hammer of hurried boots in the hall, and in the adjoining room. All four of the outlaws crowded into the kitchen.

Todd was a step ahead. He was fumbling with the buttons of his shirt, mouthing curses. "Where'n the hell did I leave my iron —" he began, then pulled up short as his sweeping glance fell upon Luke.

The others hauled up abruptly, and turned to follow his stricken gaze. Their jaws sagged, sleep-heavy, red-rimmed eyes opening wide.

"For the love of gawd!" Red muttered in an awed tone. "Where'd he come from?"

Luke motioned with his right hand gun. "Line up over there — in front of the stove.

Keep your arms up — high."

Chino and Willie crossed over slowly and took up positions near the range. Red and Todd shuffled into place beside them.

Todd said, "You get our hardware?"

Wade nodded. "You won't be needing it. I've got the rifles, too, in case you're thinking about them."

The outlaw shrugged, spat. "So you've got the drop on us. What comes next?"

"We're making a cattle drive," Wade said blandly. "We're getting that herd you rustled into the railhead by dark."

The four men stared, mouths hanging open. Then Todd laughed. "You've cut yourself one hell of a chore, bucko, if you think you can make us do that. Four to one. . . . You can't watch us all and drive cattle."

"You'll do the driving," Luke said coolly. "I'll be watching — right down the barrel of a rifle all the way. First one of you to make a wrong move gets blasted out of the saddle."

"Maybe you could try —"

"No maybe about it. I can do it — ask Red."

Todd said no more, lapsing into a sullen silence. Chino glanced toward the stove. "How about somethin' to eat?" he said, a slyness in his voice. "Long ride —"

"You'll eat when we get there — in Spilman's jail," Luke said. "Now, head out that door, single file. Your horses are at the corral."

He stepped to one side, intending to move nearer the exit. His foot caught against the leg of the chair in which he had been sitting. He went momentarily off balance, came up hard against the wall with his injured shoulder. A paroxysm of pain flashed across his face.

"He's hurt — bad!" Chino yelled. "Knew damn well we'd got him back there in the rocks!"

The rustlers halted, wheeled slowly. Wade, lips tight, rode out the hushed moments while the breathless pain gradually subsided. He wagged the pistol in his good hand menacingly.

"Keep going," he ordered. "Nothing wrong with —"

"Jump him!" Chino shouted, and lunged. A knife glittered in his fingers.

Luke took a half step back and fired from the hip. At such close quarters it was impossible to miss. The impact of the heavy bullet smashing into Chino drove the outlaw back. He thudded against the wall, eyes wide, mouth agape, and sank slowly to the floor.

Wade, watching the others through coils of acrid smoke, again moved his weapon. "Anybody else?"

There was no reply from the remaining outlaws. Luke said, "Get this straight. I've got nothing to lose — and I'd as soon kill you as take a breath after what you did to my friends back there on the flats. Now, take my advice and do what you're told. Understand?"

Red nodded sullenly. "Reckon so."

"I'm interested in one thing — getting that stock to the railhead. Help me do that and you'll get there alive. Buck me and you'll end up being buzzard bait. That's the choice you've got." He hesitated, allowing his words to sink in. Then: "We ready to pull out?"

For answer the three men wheeled and walked silently out into the yard.

XV

"Hold it!"

Luke Wade barked the command as the outlaws drew up behind their horses. It was ticklish business keeping them under close watch; at any moment they might decide to turn on him. It would be worse once the drive was under way.

"Stand pat . . . and look straight ahead!"

He wanted to be in the saddle before they mounted. Holding to both guns, and favoring his throbbing shoulder, he hauled himself onto the sorrel. Thrusting one of the pistols into his belt and holstering the other, he unslung the rifle, cocked the hammer, and laid it across his lap.

"All right," he said. "Climb aboard. Red — you drop the corral bars and let the stock out — then head them up. We're taking the shortest trail to the railhead — around the end of the mountain."

The last was a shot in the dark. He wasn't

certain such route even existed, but logically it would seem so. He watched the outlaws' expressions for a reaction that would telegraph to him that he had erred. There was none. He breathed easier. He had guessed right.

In the gray light the rustlers swung to their saddles. Red cast a sideglance at Luke, his face grim with hate, and walked his horse toward the sliding bars that closed the corral.

"You — Willie!" Wade snapped. "Ride left swing. That puts you on the right, Todd."

Todd's eyes squeezed down to slots. "Where'll you be? Trottin' along behind?"

The outlaw was thinking of the dust that ordinarily swept along in the wake of a moving herd — thick dust that could choke a man, blind him, and hide all else from him.

"I aim to be most everywhere," Luke said coolly. "Back of you — back of Willie — and looking at the back of Red's neck. Won't be one second when this rifle's not lined up on your shoulderblades."

He paused, watching the redhead push aside the poles that made up the corral's gate. "I got one more bit of good advice for you — all of you. It won't be healthy to turn around, trying to see me. You've driven cattle before, so you know what your job is.

Do it — and you'll stay alive."

The herd was beginning to stream out into the open. Red swung back onto his horse and rode forward slowly, angling toward the upper end of the hills. The lead cattle began to mill uncertainly. Wade motioned impatiently at Willie and Todd with the muzzle of his rifle.

"Get in there, damn it, and start them moving!" he snarled.

The two men wheeled in to take their assigned positions. Shouting, flaying with their ropes, they got the herd underway.

As before, there was not too much dust. The earth was covered with grass and the small number of cattle made for a minimum of disturbance. Falling in behind the swaying, bawling, heaving mass, Luke studied the thin yellow drift. It was shifting right to left. The slight breeze was out of the south. Accordingly, he angled the sorrel for that side.

Willie flung a blank look at him as he swung in close. Wade scowled and shifted the carbine. The outlaw's lips moved as he apparently swore deeply. He faced about and fell to his task.

Up ahead Luke could see Red a few yards in front of the lead steer. He was glancing neither to right nor left. Red was the one he could have the most trouble with, Wade knew. Heading up the herd, he was in the best position to make a run for freedom, since he would be at all times the farthest away.

But Luke was gambling on the redhead's reluctance to tempt death. He had backed down in Red Hill — and again at the ranchhouse. It wasn't likely he would take any chances on stopping a bullet now.

He turned his head and gazed to his left across the humping backs of the steers. Todd, slumped on his saddle, rode near the tail of the herd. He, too, was holding his eyes straight on, doing nothing more than keep pace with the cattle.

Luke slowed the sorrel, faded back into the trailing dust and spurred quickly to the opposite side. He veered in behind Todd unnoticed, and pulled up until the sorrel's bobbing head was alongside the rump of the outlaw's buckskin.

"Get the lead out of your tailend!" Luke shouted harshly. "I aim to reach the Forks by dark!"

Taken unexpectedly, Todd jumped visibly. His head swiveled about and his jaws worked furiously, but whatever he said was lost to the racket of the herd. He lifted his rope and began to fly about angrily. Several steers broke into a shambling run, and shortly the entire bunch was moving at a faster pace.

Wade recrossed the trail, and loped in behind Willie. He saw Red twist about, glance back, spot him — and quickly resume his position.

Luke sighed softly. So far, so good. He had the outlaws thoroughly buffaloed — but for how long was problematical. Later, as the day wore on, they would begin to realize they were losers regardless of what they did. As rustlers, and once in the hands of the law, they stood no chance. Under the threat of his rifle, they also could not win if they attempted an escape. It would be a hard choice.

The sun broke over the eastern horizon in a vast yellow spray of long fingers, and the coolness began to fade. By mid-morning the heat was upon them full blast, and the continual riding, the lacing back and forth, and the tension all combined to heighten the ragged pain in Luke Wade's shoulder.

He kept it hidden from the rustlers, who continued to do their jobs under his hard, relentless stare and the deadly promise of the always cocked and ready rifle. By noon they had dropped off the broad, grassy mesa and were on a second, seemingly limitless flat, but one almost barren of growth. The dust increased and maintaining a watch over the outlaws became more difficult.

Near the middle of the afternoon, sweat soaked and dust caked, his eyes smarting fiercely, his shoulder paining with a dull, maddening intensity, Luke Wade began to sense the possibility of failure. He doubted if he could maintain the constant vigilance over the outlaws for much longer. He was approaching both physical and mental exhaustion — yet he knew he could not quit, that he must get the cattle to Anson's Fork.

The reason for that had somehow become clouded in his flagging mind, and he was too worn to puzzle it out. And oddly, the primary purpose for his being in that part of the country had also gotten mislaid somewhere during the past few violent and tension-filled days. The man with the saber-scarred chest had retreated into some remote corner of his memory and had become of minor importance.

Everything centered now on the herd and its critical value to the ranchers of Mangus Valley. Of equal consideration was the need to avenge the ruthless murders of young Joe Dee Kline, of big, smiling Helm Stokes, and the quiet faced puncher, Leggett. Avenge their deaths by process of law . . . he had no desire to assume the chore of dispensing justice personally unless forced; that was up to Spilman and other authorities. He would bring the rustlers in, even aid in hunting down the remainder of the gang, but no more than that.

And here again Luke Wade was at variance with the life he had led since Ben Wade had been murdered. Vengeance had been his only goal, and the search for it had been his daily bread. The killings of Joe Dee and the other men were different, however; it was a matter for the law. Had his mind been clear enough to reason, Luke might have wondered at that fine line of differentiation he had drawn, and perhaps questioned himself.

It was late in the day when, barely able to stay upright in the saddle, he saw smoke on the horizon ahead. His hopes immediately soared, and with them also rose his strength. Only a little farther and he would have it made. Three, four miles . . . possibly less. Then the hard, murderous trip would be over, the cattle would be safe in the pens at the railhead — and the rustlers would be locked in Amos Spilman's jail.

He shifted his attention to Todd, a dozen paces to his right. He must be doubly watchful now. If the outlaws intended to make a break, it would come soon. They had little time left.

Todd felt Wade's eyes upon him, and half turned. His dust grayed face was drawn into a hard sneer. "There's your town, bucko. I'll give odds you'll never make it."

Luke's expression did not change. "I'll make it. Could be you won't."

The outlaw's lips parted in a toothy grin and he looked away. Luke held his position for several more minutes, then dropped back, circled through the trailing yellow pall, and rode in behind Willie. The rustler was hunched forward over his saddle, chin pointed straight ahead. He appeared to be watching Red, now slightly out in front of the herd . . . a little more than usual, Luke thought. Suspicion lifted swiftly within him. He spurred up to Willie's side. The outlaw swiveled about to face him.

"Whatever you're thinking — forget it!" Luke warned. "I'm close enough to that town now to get along without you — all of you!"

"Who's thinkin'?" Willie demanded with a transparent show of innocence.

"You are!" Luke shot back angrily. "Try something and I'll put a slug through you!"

Wade came about sharply as sudden

confusion on the opposite side of the herd caught the tail of his eye. He spun, and pulled away from the cattle for a better look. Through the thin edge of the pall he saw Todd, low over the saddle, cutting away, starting to make a try for the distant hills to the rear.

Luke snapped the carbine to his shoulder. He took hurried aim and pressed off a shot. The bullet dug sand immediately in front of the outlaw's horse. The buckskin shied, and reared. Luke fired again, this time purposely placing his shot as near to the outlaw's head as possible.

At the first crack of the rifle the herd began to run. Wade glanced at Willie, saw he had no problem there and swung his eyes to Red. The rustler was standing in his stirrups, his gaze on Todd as his horse broke into a lope to keep ahead of the cattle.

Luke drew close aim on the redhead. He sent a bullet whirring over his shoulder. It was so close the outlaw flinched. Instantly he dropped back onto his saddle and resumed the chore of leading the onrushing steers.

Waiting to see no more from that position, Luke raced through the dust to where he could watch Todd. The rustler had managed to bring his frightened horse under control finally. His face was working with rage and a steady flow of curses poured from his crusted, cracked lips.

"Goddam you!" he yelled as Wade rushed in. "You ain't takin' me to no lynchin'! Not me . . . you'll sure as hell have to shoot me first!"

"That's just what I figure to do!" Luke snarled, and brought up the rifle again. He took dead center aim at the outlaw.

Todd's face froze. His eyes spread, filled with fear. Abruptly he lifted his arms. "Now . . . hold on a bit," he stammered. "Wait . . . you can't . . ."

The carbine in Luke's hands did not waver. "You're the one asking for it," he said coldly. "I'll tell you same as I told Willie . . . I don't need any of you now; I can take this herd the rest of the way by myself. And nobody'd fault me if I brought in a dead rustler."

Todd settled deeper onto his saddle. He shook his head slowly. "All right, Wade. I reckon you're holdin' all the aces."

Tension began to sweep from Luke Wade's taut frame as he lowered the rifle. He had expected them to make a break for freedom and had been alert for it. It had come — and now it was over with. He had weathered the emergency.

146

He raised his eyes wearily to the east —
toward Anson's Fork. It couldn't be far now,
and the cattle, frightened by the gunshots,
were moving at a good trot. It wouldn't take
long . . .

Luke's thoughts halted. A frown crossed
his face. Three riders were approaching,
slanting in from the southeast.

Tension again rose within him. These
could be the rest of the rustling gang, the
ones Todd and the others had spoken of.
He thumbed back the hammer of the carbine, and waited.

And then, as the riders drew nearer, fad-
ing sunlight glinted upon a bit of metal
worn on the vest of one. Luke squinted
through the dry haze, and relief hit him with
sudden, joyous force. It was Amos Spilman.
With him were Bishop, the cattle buyer, and
another man he did not know.

XVI

As the gate to the maze of cattle pens at Anson's Fork swung shut, Luke Wade leaned forward and wearily laid his forearm across the horn of his saddle. That was it; the herd had been delivered. He watched as Bishop and the two men he had hastily hired on to handle the cattle made a final check of the hasps.

Satisfied that all was secure, the cattle buyer passed some silver to his assistants and then walked briskly to where Luke waited. Town Marshal Spilman and his deputy had already gone, taking their prisoners off to jail where they would remain until the arrival of the Circuit Judge.

When Bishop drew near, Luke straightened. There had been no opportunity to talk earlier; now he voiced the question that had been in his mind.

"How did it happen you and the marshal and his deputy came out to meet me?"

"We didn't," Bishop replied, leaning against the graying, unpainted cross boards of a loading chute. "I mean intentionally. Gilligan — the deputy — had a matched team he wanted to sell. I was interested, went out to see it. Spilman was along for the ride. Coming back, we heard gunshots. Headed over that way to see what it was all about. Saw it was you . . ."

"Lucky for me," Wade murmured. "I was about done in. . . . How many you tally?"

"Two hundred and eighteen. Glad now I waited for that herd. All prime stuff. I'll go top — eighteen dollars a head. Think that'll make your rancher friends happy?"

Luke nodded. "Know it will. Can we settle up now?"

Bishop smiled. "Sure, if you say so. But you're not figuring on riding back tonight, are you?"

Wade said, "Why not? No reason to hang around here. Thought I'd eat, lay around until midnight, then head out."

Bishop frowned. "Man, you're ready to fall off that horse now! And from the look on your face I'd say that shoulder of yours is giving you holy hell. Spend the night here — as my guest. Get some sleep. A few more hours aren't going to make any difference to those ranchers."

"It's not them I'm thinking about," Luke said quietly. "I want to get this chore done with. Got some business of my own to look after."

Now that the cattle were safe, the need to find the man, the killer with the saber scar on his body, had again pushed to the fore.

Bishop stared at Luke's set face for several moments. "I see," he said. "Well, it's up to you. I'll meet you in the hotel lobby in an hour."

"Good enough," Luke replied, and turned away.

He left the sorrel at the livery barn and gave instructions to rub him down good, then feed and water him, paying for the job in advance. He told the hostler he'd return around midnight.

He went then to the water trough in the yard behind the barn, stripped to the waist and washed himself thoroughly, being careful not to soak the bandage around his chest. He felt better after the cold dousing and wished it had been darker; he could then have disrobed completely and taken a bath all over. But it could wait until he reached Red Hill.

He walked the short distance to the cafe after that and spent almost the last of his available cash for a good meal. When that was over he returned to the street, and leaned back against a porch roof support to kill time until he would meet with Bishop.

Evening's coolness was setting in, and lamps in stores and nearby homes were beginning to glow. A few persons were out, strolling along the plank walks enjoying the break in the day's slashing heat. Music was issuing from several of the town's saloons, and down at the end of the street a church bell tolled the faithful to prayer services.

"Glad to see you're still kicking!"

At the sound of a familiar voice Luke wheeled. It was Dr. David. He grinned. "Thanks — but there's been times when I felt better."

"Expect so. Medically, you've got no business even being alive! Man with a hole like you've got through you ought to be in a pine box. It giving you trouble?"

"I know it's there, for damn sure," Luke said ruefully. "But I made out."

"You would. Let's step over to my office so's I can get a look at it. Bandage probably needs changing."

Wade shook his head. "Hell, Doc, I'm broke. Just spent my last —"

"No charge," David said. "Just ordinary professional interest. Goes with the original fee."

Luke grinned. "If that's the way it is, all right." It wouldn't hurt to have the wound cared for. A long ride lay ahead of him and treatment could make it less painful.

He moved off the porch that fronted the cafe and fell in beside the physician. In silence they walked down the street, heading for the doctor's combination office and residence at the far end. They reached the gate and started to turn in.

Wade halted suddenly. A rider materialized from the shadows beyond the corner of the house. Metal glinted in his hand.

"Look out!" Luke yelled and, shouldering the physician roughly into the shrubbery, he threw himself to the ground.

A gun crashed twice in quick succession, its explosion flaming bright orange in the darkness. Wood splintered just beyond Wade. He rolled fast, ignoring the pain that seared through his shoulder, drew his gun and bounded to his feet . . . too late. The rider was already hammering off into the night, offering no target.

Luke stood in angry silence, looking into the darkness into which the ambusher had disappeared. Back in the direction of town he could hear men running, coming on the double to see what all the shooting was about.

David's voice came to him from the blackness of the yard. "You hit?"

"No," Luke said, turning to the physician. "How about you?"

"Got myself a couple of scratches, that's all. Obliged to you for shoving me out of the way. Never was much hand at doctoring myself. See who it was?"

Wade shrugged, and winced at the movement. "Didn't get a good look. Happened too fast — and it was too dark."

"Well, he was no friend of yours, that's for certain. Likely one of the rustlers you didn't get."

"Must've been. I know they were waiting for one man . . . called him Jim, I think. There could be more."

Marshal Spilman, accompanied by a dozen or more townsmen, pounded up, panting for breath. The lawman's face was red.

"What's going on up here?"

"Somebody took a couple of shots at Wade," David said. "Got away before we could see who he was." The physician paused. "You right sure those three outlaws are still locked up?"

"It wasn't one of them, if that's what you're hintin' at," the lawman said, his voice rising. "I was sitting there talking to them when I heard the gunshots. He do any damage?"

"Only to my fence," David said. He glanced at Luke. "Let's go."

Wade, deep in thought, turned to follow the physician into his office. The man on the horse had to have some connection with the rustlers; it was only logical to believe he was the missing member, the one they had been waiting for.

But somehow it didn't make sense. Outlaws ordinarily weren't that faithful to their comrades in crime. They might attempt a rescue, particularly if it could be done before the jailing was complete, but to risk gunning down a man who had been no more than an instrument in their capture hardly seemed plausible. It just didn't jibe.

One thing was now certain: he'd have to leave that night as he'd originally planned. The would-be assassin could return and hang around for a second try. The sooner he got out of Anson's Fork, the better.

David found the wound to his satisfaction. He applied more ointment and a fresh bandage, and stepped back.

"Now, all you need is some rest. Take the same room you had before. Bed's ready."

Luke pulled on his shirt, smiling faintly.

"Sorry, Doc, but I've got to pull out tonight."

David smacked his hands together. "Damn it, Luke! I'd like to go around bragging about how I saved you from dying, but if you keep pushing your luck —"

"If I hang around here I'm a sitting duck for whoever that is that's pot-shooting at me. I don't feel like making it easy for him."

"Of course," the doctor said soberly. "Better keep your eyes peeled when you leave here. Probably be smart to go out the back."

"I'll do that," Wade said. "So long — and much obliged to you."

"So long," the physician said, following him onto the porch. "Take care of that shoulder."

Luke made his way down the dark alley behind the buildings until he was opposite the hotel. Then, turning into a trash littered passageway between a saloon and a harness shop, he crossed the street and entered the hostelry. From a deep leather chair in a far corner, Bishop rose to meet him. He came forward, arm outstretched.

"Glad to see you're all right!" he boomed. "Heard about the close call you had."

"Little dark out there for good shooting," Wade commented dryly. "You set to do business?"

Bishop reached into his pocket for a leather fold. He opened it and extended a draft. "All made out. Three thousand nine hundred and twenty-four dollars. You can turn it over to your friends and they can cash it anywhere. All I need now are the papers on the herd — the bills of sale."

Bills of sale!

Wade felt his spirits sink. He hadn't given the necessary papers a moment's thought. Stokes had been carrying them — likely they were still on his body. The rustlers wouldn't have troubled to take them; they would have planned to blot brands and make papers of their own.

"You've got bills of sale, haven't you?" Bishop asked, frowning.

Luke said, "Matter of fact, no. One of my partners was carrying them when he got killed. I'll have to get new ones made up."

The cattle buyer's face fell. He folded the draft and put it back in the leather fold. "Guess we'll have to put off settling up until you can get them," he said. "Matter of good business, you understand. I trust you — but my company —"

"I understand," Wade broke in, angry and impatient. More delay now faced him. It meant riding all the way to Mangus Valley, collecting new papers from the ranchers who had furnished stock for the drive — then returning to the railhead. And after that would come the long trip again to the valley.

"Any chance you riding back with me?" he suggested hopefully. "Save us both a lot of time."

Bishop laughed. "Not much. I'm no saddleman. Couple of hours on a horse and I've had enough to keep me walking for a week. . . . Besides, I'm overdue in El Paso now."

"That mean you can't wait for me to get new papers?"

Bishop scratched at his ear. "Like I said, I'm way behind now — but I guess a few more days won't make much difference. Tell you what I'll do: I'll give you a receipt for the herd, and put the draft in the bank, then I'll stall around a few more days. Anything comes up and I have to leave, just present the papers to the banker and he'll hand over the draft. That agreeable?"

"Agreeable," Luke said. "Now, if you'll just write out that receipt, I'll get on my way."

Bishop produced the leather fold once more, removed a blank sheet of paper and began to write.

"Too bad you can't take all that money

back in hard cash to your rancher friends," he said. "Expect it would sure look good to them."

No thanks, Luke thought. The unknown rider in the dark could be planning a second ambush. This time it might not fail . . . and he wasn't about to make a rich man of him, whoever he was.

XVII

The receipt for the cattle tucked into his pocket, Wade departed Anson's Fork a short time later. He had slipped out the rear entrance of *The Westerner Hotel,* hurried along a shadow filled alley and gained the livery barn unnoticed. Leaving the stable by the back, he led the sorrel through the back to the edge of the settlement and only then mounted. When he was finally on the main road west, he felt certain he had not been seen.

The weight of the long, sleepless hours bore heavily upon him now, and as the big red horse loped easily on through the silvered night, he dozed intermittently. His shoulder pained little, thanks to Doc David, and during the periods of wakefulness he planned ahead.

Soon the responsibility of the cattle would no longer be his. He had only to hand the receipt over to Travis McMahon and he was finished with it; McMahon or one of the other ranchers could make the trip to Anson's Fork and claim the money. When that was done he could resume his grim quest.

It wasn't precisely clear in his mind as to just how he would go about finding his father's killer. That it was one of the Mangus Valley ranchers he was still certain, but still, he just couldn't walk up to a man, rip open his shirt and look for a scar.

Find work on the various ranches, that was the answer. Volunteer to help out for a few days, at no wages if need be. Ranchers too poor to hire hands were always happy to furnish meals and a bed in exchange for labor. And being acquainted with most of them should make it simple.

The opportunity of looking for the saber slash would present itself; perhaps it would come while working in the open and a man peeled off his shirt to escape the heat. Or it could be at wash-up time — or possibly during a suggested swim in the creek. He'd get his chance; it would turn up. The important thing was to get started at it. He'd lost considerable time already.

The miles rocked by steadily. The sorrel, refreshed by rest and care, enjoyed the coolness and easy run. Several times he tried to increase his pace to a gallop, but Luke held him down; a long hot day faced them once the sun broke over the horizon.

He halted at dawn to ease his own stiff muscles and breathe the sorrel. While waiting he ate the last of his food, now dried to hard tack and leather, and wet it down with water.

Thirty minutes later, as he stepped back into the saddle, he threw his glance to his back trail. He was considerably south of the trail he had crossed previously with the herd, and the land was somewhat rougher and broken with low buttes and brushy arroyos.

He sat motionless on the sorrel, squinting into the rising sun while a frown pulled at his brow. Far back he could see a dark shape just below the horizon — and the thought crossed his mind that he was being followed, that he had not escaped Anson's Fork unnoticed after all. But the blurred object did not move, and Luke, finally deciding that it was a scrub cedar or pinon, rode on.

He was drawing near to the Penasco River. On the yonder side he would start watching for the bodies of Leggett and Helm Stokes. Buzzards would likely tip him off to where they lay, he realized grimly. The word of their deaths, and that of young Joe Dee

Kline, would take the edge off the good news he brought concerning the sale of the herd. Three men dead . . . the drive had been costly, even though successful.

He paused long enough at the Penasco to water the sorrel and refill his canteen, and then pushed on, his glance now alternately sweeping the broad land before him and the bright sky above. Even though the vultures and coyotes had probably gotten to them, there would be remains.

Three riders broke suddenly into view.

They appeared abruptly on the crest of a low rise far ahead, and striking east. Wary, Luke continued, his eyes fixed on the horsemen. They could be the rest of the rustlers. He grinned. He guessed he was getting overly suspicious. He had thought the same when Spilman, Bishop and the deputy had met him with the herd. Likely they were ranchers going to the Fork on business.

The trail at that point had curved farther south, and now followed along the edge of a sandy wash well studded with mesquite, rabbitbrush, creosote bush and other rank growth. He considered dropping down into the arroyo and keeping himself concealed until he had passed or was at least certain of the men.

But he didn't like the idea. It made him

feel as though he were hiding, running, and that rubbed against the grain. It was bad enough that he had had to sneak out of the settlement.

So he rode on, the three men coming into sharper focus as they drew nearer. Luke's gaze settled on the rider to his left. He frowned. There was something familiar to him, something about the way he sat his saddle. He narrowed his eyes to cut down the glare. The man in the center . . . he appeared familiar, too.

McMahon!

Surprise swept through Wade. It was McMahon on the left. Something had happened — they had gotten word of trouble and were riding to the railhead. Relief gripped Luke. It was a bit of luck he had not counted on. And then he straightened in the saddle.

"Stokes!"

The name exploded from his lips as he recognized the rider in the center of the group. The big rancher had somehow escaped the rustlers. Pleased and further relieved, he lifted his hand in salutation, and signaled them, now eyeing the third man more closely. He wasn't sure but he thought he was Joe Dee's father, Otis.

He touched the sorrel with his spurs and

163

broke him into a gallop. Immediately McMahon and the others halted. He wondered if Kline knew that his son was dead, and decided he probably did not. Stokes, making an escape, likely had been too occupied to see the boy go down. Or he could have; that would account for Otis being in the party. He could have come along to search for his son's body.

Luke waved again, lifting his hand to indicate his recognition. McMahon replied with a half-hearted gesture. Luke shrugged. His welcome was anything but cordial — and then it came to him that the men were on a sad journey. The deaths of Joe Dee and Leggett had affected them deeply.

He reached the bottom of the rise upon which the ranchers waited, and sent the sorrel trotting up the gentle grade. Gaining the top, he slanted toward them. Smiling, he bobbed his head in greeting.

"Mighty happy to see you —" he began, and stopped short. Helm Stokes, his face a curious mixture of shock and surprise, was looking at him over the barrel of a cocked revolver.

"What —"

"Climb down off that horse, you thieving bastard!" the big rancher snarled. "We've got you dead to rights!"

XVIII

Startled, Luke Wade stared at Stokes. His eyes shifted to McMahon and Otis Kline. Their faces were set, impassive. Anger lifted suddenly within him.

"What the hell's this all about?" he demanded in a rough voice.

Kline swore deeply. "He's got the guts to set there and say that! I ain't a man given to violence nowadays, but right now I could blast him off that saddle — and never take a deep breath doing it."

"Let Stokes handle it, Otis," McMahon murmured. "He knows what he's doing."

Luke's anger continued to rise. "I'll say it again — what's the trouble? You've got no call jumping me this way — not after I've worked my guts out trying to —"

"You getting off that horse, or do I shoot you off?" Helm Stokes cut in coldly. "Makes no difference to me."

Wade raised himself in his stirrups and

swung from the sorrel with great delibera-
tion. His mind was churning, seething,
struggling to understand what had happened, just what it was that had brought
about the change of attitude on the part of
the ranchers. A few days ago he had been a
friend; now he was a mortal enemy fit only
for death.

"Keep your hands up!" Stokes warned.
"And walk over here where we can watch
you."

Luke crossed in front of his sorrel, arms
uplifted. McMahon dismounted. Kline followed suit. Last of all Stokes came to
ground. Ignoring him, Wade placed his attention on McMahon; he might be his chief
suspect insofar as the murder of Ben Wade
was concerned, but he was also the man he
knew best.

"I still want to know what this means. I've
done nothing to make you throw a gun on
me —"

"He's done nothing." Stokes echoed
mockingly. "He had his bunch all lined up
to rustle our herd. He shot down Joe Dee,
left him laying out there on the flats for the
buzzards — and now he's got the nerve to
say he's done nothing!"

Struck dumb momentarily by the outra-
geous accusations, Wade simply glared at

the rancher. And then his fury boiled over.

"That's a lie — and any man who believes it is a plain fool! Sure, rustlers jumped us. They left me for dead in the Sacramentos, and drove off the stock. I got to my horse later and managed to reach the railhead. Found Joe Dee's body on the way. Figured they'd got you and Leggett, too, so I kept watching . . ." Luke paused, his eyes bright with anger. "How'd you get away?"

"They drove him off," McMahon said. "Sort of like last year. Ain't heard from Leggett. You say you've been to Anson's Fork?"

Wade nodded, again centering his attention on McMahon. The big rancher seemed interested in getting the straight of the matter.

"I was in pretty tough shape when I hit town. Somebody hauled me off to the doc's and he fixed me up and kept me in bed for a couple of nights and a day. But quick as I was able, I headed back this way. Figured the herd had to be around here somewhere."

As he spoke Wade's temper began to cool. McMahon and the others had things all wrong somehow. It was up to him to clear it up.

"Finally located the stock at a ranch on the upper end of the Penasco. Four men were looking after them. Had a bit of trouble with one, but I made the others drive the herd on in to Anson's Fork. Buyer by the name of Bishop was waiting. He took the lot."

McMahon's jaw sagged. "You got the cattle to the railhead — and sold them?"

"Just the way we figured —"

"You're a fool to listen to that!" Stokes said harshly. "Nothing but hogwash. He's stringing up — trying to save his own neck." The rancher paused and looked up, his eyes reaching to the flat beyond Luke. The faint, rhythmic beat of an oncoming horse hung in the calm, heat-charged air.

"You mentioned my boy," Kline said gently. "His body — where's it now?"

"Waiting for you at Anson's Fork," Luke replied. "Marshal took charge . . . I'm sorry, Mr. Kline. Wasn't anything I could do for him. He was already dead."

Kline bowed his head. "However this turns out, I'm obliged to you for not leaving him laying out there."

"I didn't shoot him. It was one of the rustlers. Could have been the one I had trouble with at that ranch. Or it could have been one of the others. There's three of them in jail now at the railhead."

The approaching hoofbeats grew louder. McMahon, shading his eyes with his hand

and squinting, said, "Say, that looks like your man Leggett, Stokes."

Surprise again rushed through Luke. Both Stokes and Leggett alive! Only he and Joe Dee had dropped under the rustler's guns.

Stokes said, "It sure is him! Now, maybe we can get the straight of this. Expect what he'll tell us will prove Wade's a damned liar."

"It's no lie," Luke said softly. A calmness had settled over him as a vague suspicion began to grow. "I can back up everything I've told you."

"Oh, sure," Stokes said in an offhand, crooked grin way. "Your kind always has ways of proving things. People that'll swear they saw you —"

"I've got the receipt for the herd," Wade cut in unhurriedly in a quiet voice.

Stokes' face hardened. His words died in his throat as his brow pulled into deep corrugations.

A smile began to spread across Travis McMahon's lips. "A *receipt,* you say!"

"Right. There's a draft waiting for you at the bank. I couldn't get it because I didn't have the papers on the herd."

There was a long moment of silence and then McMahon boomed, "By God — can't be no better proof than that! Stokes, you're all wrong somewhere. Let me see that receipt, Luke."

Shifting his glance to Stokes, still covering him with his pistol, Wade dug into his right hand pocket and procured the fold of paper given him by Bishop. He extended it toward McMahon.

"That cattle buyer's in a hurry to move on. You ought to —"

"I'll take that!" Stokes snapped, and grabbed the receipt from Luke's fingers. He whirled about, and abruptly stood facing all three men. "You won't be needing it."

McMahon's beefy face flushed. "Now, what the hell does this —"

"Just stand tight," Stokes said. "And keep your hands in front of you. Leggett'll be here in a couple more minutes and we'll wind this little shindig up."

Understanding came then to Luke Wade. Stokes and Leggett were both in on the rustling. Jim Leggett . . . Jim . . . that was the name Todd and the other outlaws had mentioned, the man they were waiting for. Stokes was probably the leader of the bunch. He swore, angered by his own blindness. Why hadn't he been able to see it?

Otis Kline found his voice. "You mean you're the one who's been stealing our stock?" he asked in an unbelieving tone. "It — it was you last year?"

Stokes smiled. "You guessed it, Otey. It was me. Had myself a pretty good thing going. . . . Still would have," he added, flicking a glance at Luke, "if my boys had done the job on him they were supposed to."

"But Joe Dee — a boy. Why did you —"

"Real sorry about that. Tried to scare the kid off, but he wouldn't run. I couldn't have him carrying tales, so one of the boys had to take care of him."

A deep sob broke from Kline's throat. McMahon, his words cold and squarely spaced, said, "You're the worst kind of a sonofabitch, Stokes! Making out like you were a friend, letting us trust you while all the time you were robbing and killing —"

"Forget it, Travis!" the rustler snarled. "No need to get all riled up. You won't have to stew over it much longer."

"Meaning what?"

"One thing, of course," Stokes said. Behind him Leggett had pulled out of the arroyo and halted. "Come on up here, Jim," he called, not turning his head.

Leggett, leading his horse, moved in. McMahon asked again, "Meaning what?"

"Now, I can't just leave you three running loose, can I? I'd be a damned fool to do that."

Kline's voice showed no fear, only surprise. "You aim to kill us?"

"Got to, Otey. Hate it, but I got no choice."

Luke listened in silence. He was calculating the odds, trying to find an opening somehow. But Leggett's arrival had complicated and narrowed the chances.

"How you going to explain this to the people waiting back in the valley?" McMahon said. "Us just dropping out of sight's going to be hard to cover up."

"Don't figure to," Stokes said. "Nothing left around here for me now — not the way it worked out this year. I'll just ride on in to Anson's Fork, hand over this receipt and the papers I'm carrying, and collect the money. Then I'll move on."

"*We'll* move on," Jim Leggett corrected quietly, coming up behind Stokes and halting by the tall man's shoulder. "Things sure have blowed up."

"They have — thanks to you," Stokes replied angrily. "We could have strung it out for a couple or three more years if you hadn't bungled the job. How's it happen you didn't take care of this saddlebum?"

"We did!" Leggett said protestingly. "Hit him twice while he was up there in the rocks. Then next thing I knew, there he was in the Fork. Tried again when I got the

172

chance, but it was too dark and I missed. I hung around, looking for him, but he snuck out of town. Followed fast as I could . . ."

"Well, no matter now. I've got what we need to claim the money. Next thing's to get rid of these three. Over there in that arroyo ought to be a good spot. Then we'll pick up the cash and head north."

Travis McMahon shook his head. "You'll never get away with it, Stokes. It's cold-blooded murder you're talking — and a lot of people know we rode out together."

"And we're all disappearing together," Stokes said with a broad smile. "You think of that? Something happened to all of us, that's what people'll think. I've got everything figured down to a hair, Travis. That's one reason why I've got by all these years — I figure ahead."

He turned to Luke. "And you, cowboy — I don't know where you got that gun, but I want it. It's mine."

XIX

Cold rage soared through Luke Wade. He forced himself to remain calm.

"Your gun? What makes you think so?"

"Spotted it first time I laid eyes on you. Got lost a couple years ago up Wyoming way. Had me some trouble with a crusty old codger who tried slicin' me in two with a saber, and I dropped it somehow . . ."

"You're — him!" Luke yelled, and, heedless of all else, he lunged at the killer who for so long had been but a dim shadow before him.

The outlaw's gun roared in his ears. He felt the hot slash of the bullet as it seared across his rib cage. But he knew no pain — only a surging exultation as his clawing fingers encircled Stokes' neck. Guns blasted — twice. There was no sickening impact. Vaguely, he realized it wasn't Stokes' weapon that had fired.

"I been hunting you — years!" Luke heard

his own voice shouting. "That was my pa you murdered . . . an old man . . . crippled up . . . couldn't protect himself. I swore on his grave I'd track you down and make you pay!"

His flaming mind became aware that Stokes had collapsed beneath him; that he was kneeling on the outlaw's chest choking him; that his shoulder was screaming with pain.

He became aware, too, of hands dragging at him, pulling him off. Travis McMahon's voice dinned into his consciousness.

"Luke! Luke! Let him go. Save him for the hangman!"

Gasping for breath, Wade staggered back. Pain was writhing through him like a thing alive. He sagged against the sorrel. The yellow haze that filled his eyes began to fade and he looked about. Leggett lay on the sandy earth, glazed eyes staring into the hot sky. A broad, red stain covered his breast.

Those were the gunshots he had heard. McMahon, or Kline, had taken care of Leggett. He shifted his glance to Stokes, now stirring weakly. The outlaw's mouth was gaped, and he made dry, rasping sounds as he struggled for breath. Luke swayed to him, leaned over. He grasped the man's shirt front in his trembling hand and ripped it open. The long, thin mark of Ben Wade's saber ran the full length of his torso.

Hate and anger burst again through Wade. He drew back a stride. The ornate pistol — the killer's own gun at his hip — came swift and smooth into his hand.

"Got to kill him," he murmured in a tight voice. "He's got to die . . . can't trust it to the law. . . ."

McMahon's words were low and soothing. "Easy now, boy. Reckon I understand now what's been bothering you. Don't say as I blame you for how you feel — but don't make the mistake of killing him."

"It's no mistake," Luke said woodenly.

"Your doing it would be. This vengeance hunt you've been on for so long wouldn't die with him . . . not really. It'd keep right on living, because you'd keep on thinking how you'd killed him, how you'd finally squared things for your pa . . . and it'd be the wrong kind of satisfaction.

"It's not the good kind, because down deep you'd know all the time you were a murderer, too — no better'n him. . . ."

"Listen to him, son," Otis Kline said quietly. "He's talking gospel, pure gospel. I know . . . I been through it."

"Let the law finish it for you," McMahon said. "Then you'll sleep easy the rest of your time. And the law'll do it — you've got my guarantee. I'll see him right up to the gallows. Expect Otey'll give you the same promise."

"You can bet on it," Kline said in a hard voice. "He owes me, too — for Joe Dee. . . ."

Luke Wade looked down at the weapon in his hand. It no longer was the sleek, efficient bit of beauty it had always seemed — no longer the symbol of what he had to do. Now it was a heavy, ugly machine of death — the very one that had snuffed out his father's life. Suddenly he wheeled, and hurled the weapon off into the loose sand of the arroyo.

"I reckon it's finished," he said wearily. He stepped back and pointed at Stokes. "Let's get him to the Fork and hand him over to the marshal."

McMahon's thick shoulders settled in relief. He smiled. "Figured I wasn't wrong about you. If you've got no place special you're aiming to go, how about coming back to the valley? Expect folks would be right pleased to help you get started — and the country can always use a good cattleman."

"You'd be welcome to move in with us," Kline added. "Got an empty room now, and — and I could use a son. . . ."

Luke felt a lump rise in his throat. He was

silent for a long minute, then: "Obliged to you both. . . . Sure would be fine, tying down to one place again."

Real fine, he added to himself — *with Samantha close by. . . .*

We hope you have enjoyed this Large Print book. Other Thorndike, Wheeler, Kennebec, and Chivers Press Large Print books are available at your library or directly from the publishers.

For information about current and upcoming titles, please call or write, without obligation, to:

Publisher
Thorndike Press
10 Water St., Suite 310
Waterville, ME 04901
Tel. (800) 223-1244

or visit our Web site at:

http://gale.cengage.com/thorndike

OR

Chivers Large Print
published by AudioGO Ltd
St James House, The Square
Lower Bristol Road
Bath BA2 3SB
England
Tel. +44(0) 800 136919
email: info@audiogo.co.uk
www.audiogo.co.uk

All our Large Print titles are designed for easy reading, and all our books are made to last.